A Stolen Chance

by

Linda LaRoque

A Stolen Chance

Cover Art by *Diana Carlile*

The Wild Rose Press, Inc.
PO Box 708
Adams Basin, NY 14410-0708
Visit us at www.thewildrosepress.com

Publishing History
First Faery Rose Edition, 2013
Digital ISBN 978-1-61217-625-3
Print ISBN 978-1-62830-126-7

Published in the United States of America

Chapter One

"I'm coming for you, darling."

Susan Lawton gasped, terror choking off any possible sound. *How had he gotten her number?*

"Cat got your tongue?" His evil snicker carried across the phone line. Then his voice sobered. "Don't worry. You'll find your voice when I arrive. And I will come for you, never fear. This time I'll make sure you're dead."

His breath rasped, echoing memories of his hot, wet mouth against her ear, uttering ugly insults. She shuddered.

"I hear you've dropped my name. The name Holt not good enough for you, huh? Tsk, tsk. Another black mark against you, my dear."

A maniacal laugh echoed through the receiver. Susan jumped and jerked the phone away from her ear. *Click.* A dial tone hummed. Her breathing rapid, she willed herself to calm down, to stop shaking. For eight years she'd plotted, preparing for this day. She couldn't—no, she wouldn't—let her fear of her ex-husband paralyze her. Calmly, she placed the handset on the charger. From across the room, her reflection in the hall mirror stared back at her. The new face, the one Doctor Scott had reconstructed from the mess Dewayne left her after his last vicious attack, became more familiar each day. Though the external scars had faded, the internal ones were still vivid, etched in her mind forever.

She mentally shook herself, grabbed the phone, and dialed her friend and co-conspirator, Lauren. Lauren picked up on the third ring. Susan didn't let her speak but blurted out their agreed-upon code, "Pizza party Monday night. You bring my favorite, and I'll provide the wine and dessert."

There was a pause on the other end. They'd discussed this day for two years, made preparations, and developed this system in case Dewayne had somehow tapped her phone. With his connections, anything was possible. That the time had arrived seemed surreal and left Susan breathless as she waited for Lauren's response.

"O...kay. Can I bring anything else?"

"No, I think that'll do it." Susan struggled to not cry. She glanced at the ceiling. A tiny spider dangled from a single strand of silk, apparently oblivious to its precarious position. Oh, to be so trusting and self-assured. "Thank you, girlfriend. You're the best."

****

Dewayne Holt huddled deeper into his coat and tucked his chin to his chest to ward off the cold. He'd driven past the isolated house, turned around, and pulled the truck he'd borrowed off the road so he could watch Susan's comings and goings. She'd sure as hell screwed up, buying this secluded property. The small house sat in the middle of a large, grass-covered lot. A few trees dotted the front lawn. A multitude of pines covered the property line at the back. Anyone could sneak up on her unseen. No nearby neighbors and no street lights.

He smirked. The small Cape Cod was an insult. Susan had received their five-bedroom Tudor in the divorce settlement. She could've bought three houses nicer than this dump. He couldn't wait to find out why she'd resorted to living in poverty.

Lights approached. Fog obscured the truck windows. He used his elbow to clear a spot and watched an old Ford Taurus pull into Susan's drive. What a pile of junk. A woman got out of the car. The wind caught long dark hair and whipped strands around her face as she struggled to balance a box of pizza and an oversized shoulder strap purse. He snorted. Women and their baggage. Enough room in that thing to store a week's change of clothes. Damn. Surely she didn't intend to spend the night. He wanted to get this over with. He'd waited too long for this moment. While he rotted away in prison, the vision of Susan's eyes bulging as he choked the life out of her had kept him from going crazy. Revenge would be sweet, and then maybe he could go on with his life, what was left of it.

The front door opened. He snatched a pair of binoculars from the seat beside him while lowering the window. He trained the glasses on the entranceway. His breath rushed from his chest. He'd dreamed of this day for eight long years. Ah, yes, there she was. She'd cut her hair to chin length. Susan laughed and held the door for her friend to squeeze past her. He gulped. She'd been beautiful before, but the plastic surgeon's talented knife had made her more so. When he'd left, she'd been just a girl. Now she was a woman. Generous breasts pushed against a blue sweater. His groin tightened and raged to life at the thought of squeezing those soft mounds while pounding into her unwilling flesh. He groaned and adjusted his uncomfortable length. Bitch. Maybe he'd enjoy her one last time.

What a shame she had to die. He'd loved her once, but not any longer. No woman testified against him, sent him to the pen, and lived to tell about it.

****

Susan's smile melted the minute she closed the door. Her voice trembled. "Did you see him?"

Lauren walked into the small kitchen and placed the square box on the dinette table. She dropped her purse into a chair, took off her coat, and folded the wool garment across the back. "Yes, parked down the road, facing this way, in an older model dark pickup truck."

"He's been there about an hour. I hope he's freezing his balls off." Susan tried to pour them a glass of wine, but she shook so badly the red liquid slopped onto the counter.

Lauren took the bottle from her. "I'll do this. You get the plates and napkins."

A giggle erupted from Susan's mouth. It turned into a sob. "I'm sorry. I'm a nervous wreck. What if I can't follow through with this?"

"Stop it. You have to, and you will." Lauren had been her strength these past few years as they'd planned and plotted. "Come on. Let's sit down and eat."

The aroma of pepperoni and Italian spices filled the air. Susan's stomach lurched from the heavy odors. "I'm not sure I can." They both sat, occupying spots they'd designated as their own after months of eating together at Susan's small table.

"You don't have a choice. It may be hours before you have a chance to stop and get food."

"You're right." She lifted her glass. "A toast. To the best friend a woman ever had."

"Ditto," said Lauren, smiling as she added, "and to a new beginning for you."

They clinked glasses and drank. The strong red wine eased Susan's nerves somewhat, and she forced down two slices of pizza. She chewed and swallowed each bite with care, fearing it might lodge in her throat.

Twenty minutes later Lauren removed the dark wig from her head to reveal bleached blonde hair styled the same way as Susan's own. Susan took the wig and, before her bathroom mirror, adjusted the long dark strands until it appeared to be her own hair. In the kitchen, she slipped into Lauren's heavy coat and fitted the gigantic purse over her shoulder. Her handbag with Susan Lawton's identification inside hung from a chair back in the kitchen. Dressed in jeans and tennis shoes identical to those Lauren wore, she looked around her home one last time. The house had been a haven, a place she'd chosen because it held no tie to Dewayne. Though not fancy, it was comfortable and suited her style. She'd miss it.

She wasn't ready to go, to leave her friend and all she knew. Fear, grief, and loneliness choked her. She wanted to scream and vent her frustration at being forced to run—but she didn't have a choice. If Dewayne didn't kill her, he'd never leave her alone and would make her life miserable. Restraining orders hadn't kept him away before, nor would one now.

It was time. She took a deep breath and turned to Lauren. They walked into each other's arms. "I'll miss you." Struggling to stem her tears, Susan squeezed her friend tightly and then stepped back. "You'll text when you get home tonight, right? I'll worry until I know you're out of danger. When Dewayne discovers I'm gone, he'll harass you to find out where I am. I couldn't bear it if he hurt you."

Lauren's friendship had been a lifesaver for Susan. She'd been the support Susan needed during her recovery. Her parents were too close to look at the situation without letting their emotions get involved. She was their baby, and she didn't want them to worry about details. They knew she planned to flee, but not exactly when and how. Her father would kill Dewayne if he hurt her again. Not that she'd mourn the man's loss, but she didn't want murder on her father's conscience, nor did she want him to go to prison. And she wouldn't put it past Dewayne to kill both her parents. The man was evil.

She'd tried to talk her folks into leaving the country, taking a trip to Europe. They wouldn't even discuss it. They'd finally conceded to allowing her to hire a bodyguard to live in their home, posing as an out-of-work nephew. Knowing her father, the poor man would earn his keep while hanging around their house.

Though Lauren cared about Susan, she wasn't wrapped up in Susan and Dewayne's past the way her folks were. Lauren could view the situation with less emotion. She'd seen Dewayne's handiwork, but not the numerous times her parents had, plus she'd never known him. Lauren was the best friend she'd ever had. Susan loved her like a sister.

"Don't worry about me. I'll be long gone before he discovers you're not here." They'd planted a car on the dirt road behind the pines that bordered her back yard. While Susan left by the front door, Lauren would leave through the back. Lights were on timers so it would appear Susan had gone to bed. They figured that's when Dewayne would make his move. Hopefully she'd be miles down the highway by then.

"How can I ever thank you, repay you for helping me?"

Lauren sniffled and shoved Susan toward the door. "By staying out of that bastard's clutches, that's how. Now, get out of here. Enjoy this adventure, but don't let your guard down."

Susan nodded and took a deep, calming breath before opening the door. Her legs wobbled as she walked outside and got into the old car she'd picked out a year ago. The Taurus hummed to life when she turned the key. The vehicle might look like a heap, but it ran like a top. She backed out of the drive and shot a quick glance at Dewayne to make sure he remained put. She was alone on the street. Her headlights wove a path down the tree-lined darkened roadway. Branches resembled seeking arms waiting to nab any unsuspecting traveler. She shivered, turned up the heat, and focused on keeping the car on the road.

A half hour later, constantly checking her rearview mirror, praying Dewayne wasn't behind her, she reached the outskirts of Chicago.

She breathed a sigh of relief and followed the Interstate around until she could pick up old Route 66. It ran through Cicero, home of Chicago mobsters during Prohibition, where the area was riddled with tunnels. If only she could move with as much stealth as the bootleggers had while fleeing the police or Elliot Ness and his Untouchables.

Her new cell phone, the one she'd purchased with

her new identity, chimed. She had an instant message. *Please, God, let Lauren be safe.* She grabbed her phone off the passenger seat. *Home safe. L.* Susan released the breath she hadn't realized she was holding. *Thank you, Lord.* She grinned. They'd outfoxed old Dewayne. Her smile wilted. Dewayne might be clueless right now, but he'd be after her as soon as he discovered she'd run. *Don't let down your guard, Susan.*

Just outside of Joliet, she turned onto a gravel country road. Dust and tiny rocks flew out behind her vehicle as she traversed the dark country lane for six miles to an old rundown barn. The structure and ten surrounding acres belonged to her. Her low beams spotlighted the winter grass covering the ruts and hiding evidence of her previous trips. She parked several yards away from the barn, killed the engine and lights, and got out of the car. Freezing air struck her in the face. She pulled her collar closer around her neck and ran to the double doors. Using the key on her key chain, she opened the padlock. Why she'd bothered locking the dilapidated entrance was a mystery, as a swift kick would have loosened the hasp. The appearance of being secure had eased her mind.

The small camper van she'd purchased several months ago sat inside. On previous trips, she'd stocked it with food, clothes and toiletries, reading material, and drugstore remedies for colds and minor aches. Weekly visits to start the motor kept the battery charged. With her flashlight, she searched the ground for critters as she walked toward the vehicle. She unlocked the cab, started the engine, and backed out of the building. She left it running while she moved the car inside, leaving the keys in the ignition. If someone broke in and took the Taurus, they were welcome to the small sedan. Closing the barn doors, she added the padlock to the hasp and snapped it in place.

Inside the van, she rubbed her hands together in front of the air vent to warm up. *Okay, Susan... Oops! Her name was Shannon, Shannon Langley, from now on.* Thanks to an unsavory connection of Lauren's, she had new identification in her purse and in the glove box as proof. The papers weren't easy to come by—had cost a small fortune, in fact—but she'd been willing to pay whatever necessary to obtain them. She'd received a decent settlement from Dewayne in the divorce and couldn't think of a better use for the funds. He'd roar with fury to discover he'd help finance her escape. Her parents had begged her to approach the FBI and ask to be in the witness protection program, but with her luck Dewayne would have an informant on the inside. More to the point, she felt sure he did. She'd not take a chance.

She took a deep breath. *Steady, girl. It's now or never.* She threw the van into reverse, backed up, and then shifted again and drove forward, away from the barn. Through her rearview mirror, she watched the structure grow smaller as she severed the last tie with Susan Lawton's past.

****

Dewayne waited, counting the minutes, for an entire hour after the Taurus left Susan's house. He slid from the pickup and, hunched over, ran down the road, staying to the shadows. He looked over his shoulder—no one there. He scurried across the lawn to the back of the house. Light shone from one window. It illuminated a patch of dry grass. He edged around the window frame to peer inside. Sheer curtains masked his view somewhat, but without a doubt, at the kitchen table in front of a laptop computer, sat the bitch that'd sent him to prison. Head down on her forearms, she appeared to be asleep. Or drunk. An empty wine bottle sat on the table, an almost full glass at her elbow.

His body shook as he struggled to restrain his mirth. Caught her unawares. He stepped onto the porch and inspected the doorknob. Stupid woman didn't even have sense enough to install deadbolt locks. With his pocket knife, he inserted the blade between the door and the jamb, carefully jiggled the knob, and felt the bolt give. He shoved the door open. Susan didn't budge. The rotten smell of sulfur hit him in the face. A loud snap, a whoosh, a burst of flame...

Chapter Two

Light exploded in his face. A force lifted and propelled him out the door. He landed on his back, twenty feet from the house, with a loud thud knocking the breath out of him. Shit. What'd happened? Smoke rose off his clothes and grew to tongues of flame. He slapped at his body to extinguish the fire licking at him as he screamed. *My hands, oh God, my hands!* He touched his face and shrieked. Horror stole what little air he had in his lungs. *The bitch has disfigured me.* His face and hands... The aroma of burnt flesh filled his nostrils. Nausea rolled in his stomach. His eyes stung. He whimpered. Was he blind? He squinted and through a cloudy fog watched as flames shot from the door and window of the kitchen. The entire house would be engulfed within minutes. Susan couldn't have survived such an inferno. Damn, the bitch had screwed him once again.

Coughing, gasping for air, Dewayne rolled to his feet. Through a haze, he stared at the fire as he staggered toward his pickup, wincing with each step. The cold winter wind against his inflamed skin drew a groan from his throat. *I have to get out of here.* The fire department would be here soon.

He struggled to get the truck door open. It hurt like hell. By the time he got inside, tears were rolling down his face. Thank God he'd left the keys in the ignition.

Gritting his teeth, he grasped the key and turned. He shuddered at the pain and drew in deep gulps of air. *Don't faint, man.* The engine turned over and started. He curved his arm around the gear shift, put it in drive, and then spun gravel in his hurry to get away undetected. Hell, if caught in the area, they'd blame the explosion on him and send him back to prison. *No shit, Sherlock. If you killed her, they'd know it was you who done it and send you back to the joint.* But he'd had a plan all laid out, an alibi, one that was foolproof. Guess he didn't need it now.

Struggling to see, he slowed down and gained control of the skidding vehicle. Hunched over the steering wheel, he fought his near blindness to stay on the road. His head swam, blackness threatened. He shook himself to stay alert. As he moved along at a crawl, flashing lights and blaring sirens raced toward him. He pulled over onto the shoulder to allow the fire trucks to pass. Pain shot to his brain as the bright rays seared his eyeballs. He threw his hand up to protect against the glare. Nausea choked him, and he gritted his teeth to ward off the sensation. Sweat rolled off his body, dampening his clothes. He shivered and turned up the heater. When all the vehicles had passed, he eased back onto the road.

He needed medical help fast, but no way could he go to a hospital. With his record and the explosion of his ex-wife's house, the police would be on him before he had time to take a pain pill. There was only one man in the area with the power to provide prompt, discreet treatment—Leo Sharp, Dewayne's past employer and one of Chicago's crime bosses.

Dewayne would owe him, big time.

****

Carson Rhodes drove into the parking lot of Albuquerque's downtown police department. He sat for a moment and looked on the familiar scene. Regret filled him. This was his last trip to his workplace. Fifteen years down the drain. He sighed and patted Hans, his German shepherd. The dog turned intelligent brown eyes on Carson and nudged him sympathetically. "I'm okay, boy. You stay put. I'll be back." He lowered the windows a fraction, just enough for some fresh air to invade the truck cab, and locked the doors.

The cold January air nipped at his ears, and he pulled the collar up to block some of the chill. Inside, as he walked to his chief's office, the room hummed with activity. Phones rang and officers hauled cursing drunks to holding cells while others took reports from victims. Captain Farley sat behind his desk, bent over a stack of paperwork, sleeves rolled up to expose bulging forearms. He looked up as Carson laid his badge and gun on Captain Farley's desk.

The burly captain, expression grim, scooped them up, placed them in an open drawer, and shoved it closed. "I hope you've made the right decision, Rhodes."

"I have, Captain." He offered his hand.

Captain Farley stood, clasped it with his meaty paw, and shook vigorously. "All right, then. If you change your mind, we'll be here."

"I don't expect that to happen, but I'll keep your offer in mind." Carson started for the door but stopped and turned. "If you ever get any time off, I know a quaint little motel in Siesta that offers rooms by the week, cheap."

The big man snorted. "I haven't had a vacation in five years. Do yourself a favor and don't hold a room for me." He waved. "Get out of here before you get caught in five o'clock traffic."

Carson chuckled as he walked from the building into the brisk forty-five-degree weather. Hans woofed in greeting as Carson opened the driver's-side door of the F150 pickup and slid into the cab.

"Hey, Hans, ol' boy. You ready to head home?"

Tongue lolling, tail beating a rhythm on the seat, Hans yipped happily.

"Yeah, me too."

The truck started instantly, and he eased out into traffic. He headed north on Rio Grande Boulevard, and when he reached I-40, he turned west. It would take almost three hours to reach Siesta, the small town halfway between Gallup and Thoreau. He'd visited often as a child. Now it would be his home.

Ten years ago his grandfather had passed away and left Carson a small travel court and restaurant on old Route 66. His aunt and uncle had been managing the Siesta Inn for years and now begged for a reprieve. He planned to give it to them.

After his accident on the job, one he couldn't put behind him, he'd decided to leave the force. Counseling had helped, but in his sleep he still saw the life drain from that little girl's eyes. He shuddered and directed his thoughts to the Siesta Motel and Café. It was time for Carson to step up and take over the business. He'd worked there during the summers until going off to college, so he knew the management process. Gramps had seen to it.

He'd thought of selling the place, but feared

Grandpop's ghost would haunt him. He grinned at the tales his mother, aunt, and uncle had told. Apparently they believed Grandpop, Carson's great-grandfather, couldn't rest and haunted the motel looking for some treasure he'd hidden and not revealed before his untimely death in 1974. No one knew exactly what the treasure was, but Gramps said the Great Spirit came to him in a dream telling him he must help his people save face. His mother and Aunt Leona always believed that story was merely the ramblings of an old man, one whose mind wasn't as sharp as it had once been. Carson considered their attitude insulting to his grandfather. He remembered Gramps as a quick-witted individual, one finely in tune with his surroundings and his Native American culture. If the spirits of his Laguna heritage spoke through him, that was fine with Carson. He'd felt the Spirit's pull himself from time to time.

Just after eight p.m. the neon lights of the Siesta Motel and Café came into view. The vintage sign, a red sombrero below a green-and-brown palm tree with a blue moon behind, greeted him like an old friend. That it still worked properly amazed Carson. Most of the old advertisements along Route 66, as well as the properties they'd promoted, were broken, mere shells of their former glory. He drove into the parking lot, passed the café and registration office, and pulled into the small garage beside cabin number six. It'd been the innkeeper's lodgings since his grandfather built it in the late 1960s. A light glowed inside. Aunt Leona no doubt had the place spotless and well-stocked with supplies for his arrival.

He got out, grabbed his duffle bag, and called Hans out of the truck. At a lope, the dog headed for the scrub brush area on the north side of the building, stopping to sniff and mark his territory. Tomorrow would be soon enough for Hans to explore. Tonight Carson wanted something to eat, a beer, and bed.

"Take care of business, boy, and come right back."

Hans raised his head and then searched with purpose. Carson stuffed his hands in his pockets and breathed in the cold, clean desert air. Stars dotted the dark open expanse above him, reminding him of his smallness in this great universe. Having given up what he'd known and loved doing for the past fifteen years, he felt particularly alone. He'd adjust, given time. He sighed. Nothing like the scents of the desert to heal the soul. He could hope, anyway.

Hans returned and sat at his feet.

"All right, boy, let's take a look at our new home." He opened the unlocked door, stepped inside, and flipped on the overhead light. The old furniture sported new covers, and the linoleum on the floors had been replaced. Even with the changes, a subtle scent of his grandfather's pipe tobacco lingered in the air. The place brought back memories of fun summers spent with Gramps. He'd worked days in the café, scrubbing floors and waiting tables. As a teen, he'd learned to flip burgers and cook breakfast. Some nights, he and Gramps camped out in the fields behind the motel, where tales of spirit talkers and *nukpanas*, evil spirits, filled his head, interfering with his sleep. He'd loved his grandfather, and the familiar space wrapped around him like open arms. For a moment he half expected Gramps to walk out from the bedroom.

The aroma of spicy food hit his nostrils. His stomach growled in protest. Hans lifted his head, nose twitching in interest.

"Sorry, buddy. I'm sure Aunt Leona laid in some chow for you. I'm not going to share Uncle Buck's Mexican stew."

Fifteen minutes later, Carson savored his uncle's spicy dish with corn cakes while Hans crunched on his dry dog food. He didn't miss the expression of reproach his furry friend shot him while he chewed. Carson ignored the mutt. Some things a man just didn't share. Plus, the highly seasoned food would play havoc on the dog's intestinal tract. He didn't want to be getting up in the wee hours for Hans to go out. He took a hefty slug of beer and let the icy brew cool his burning throat.

When he was finished with the meal, Carson stood and carried his dishes to the sink, where he rinsed and stacked them to wash tomorrow after breakfast. His jacket lay across the back of the sofa. He grabbed it, stuffed his arms into the sleeves, and then opened the door. "Come on, boy. One more trip outside."

Hans loped out the door and made for the bushes that bordered the drive.

Later, stretched out on the bed, Carson tossed and turned trying to get comfortable. The mattress must be older than his thirty-eight years. He'd buy a new one first chance he got, queen-sized, as the double didn't accommodate his six-foot height. How Gramps had managed to get a decent night's rest was a wonder, since the man had stood two inches taller than his grandson. Carson finally found a spot on his side, knees drawn up in a curled position. Hans, on the rug beside the bed, sighed deeply.

He'd just dozed off when a sound woke him. Moonlight outlined Hans standing by the bed looking at the doorway. The ruff on his neck and back stood on end. A low throaty growl rumbled from his throat.

His voice a soft whisper, Carson asked, "What's the matter, boy?" He peered into the moonlit room and didn't see a thing, but he trusted Hans. He reached out and touched the dog's flank. Hans sat. Carson eased from the bed and reached for the Smith and Wesson .38 revolver he'd placed on the bedside table. His bare feet touched the cold floor as he moved from the rug to the other room and flipped on the light. His eyes scoured the dark corners but found nothing. He lowered the gun.

"Nobody here, Hans. You must have been dreaming. Come on, look for yourself."

Hans trotted into the room and searched, seeking his dream's scent. Carson laughed, but paused in mid guffaw when Hans barked, and with front paws on the table, sniffed at a small object.

Damn. Where'd that come from? He'd wiped the table down after eating. He'd have seen it if it had been there then.

Carson picked up the tiny stone and held it in the palm of his hand. He had to examine it carefully to decide what it was, but with the protrusion of the tiny beak and a turquoise eye, he concluded it was a miniature black raven, a Zuni symbol for magic and great mystery. He stared down at the table. Grains of cornmeal were scattered around where the fetish had sat—food for its journey.

****

The clock on the dashboard read just after two a.m. Still in Illinois, Susan stopped at a large truck stop on the outskirts of Pontiac, where she filled up with gas and retreated to the back of her camper van to the porta-potty closet. Though tempted to visit the restaurant inside, she resisted, afraid she'd show up on the security cameras. After cleaning her hands with disinfectant wipes, she grabbed a soda from the mini fridge and snacks from the cupboard. In the driver's seat, she fished through Lauren's monster purse in search of one of the sandwiches her friend had provided for the trip.

Two stops to stretch her legs and almost five hundred miles later, Susan reached the outskirts of Joplin, over halfway across Missouri. A billboard advertising an RV park caught her eye. She turned into the tree-studded entrance and stopped at the park office. Ten minutes later she pulled into space number fifteen, far from view of the highway. Getting her van connected to the utilities didn't take long, a skill she and Lauren had perfected while camping. With the expandable roof cranked up, Susan could stand easily. While heating a can of tomato soup on the two-burner butane stove, she munched on a ham-cheese-and-lettuce sandwich.

Her appetite satisfied, Susan eyed her bed, tired beyond measure and longing to crawl into the sleeping bag and fall into oblivion. Instead, she grabbed a towel, her toiletries, and a pair of sweats. She locked the van and walked two spaces down to the bathhouse. She'd sleep better after a warm shower.

Full, clean, and warm, Susan curled onto her side in her sleeping bag. Though her body cried out for sleep, her brain ran rampant, sorting through files of past hurts and escape plans. At the moment, she rode an emotional high. After all, she'd left Dewayne behind, a major accomplishment. Would she crash and fall in a few days? She'd left her parents and friends—well, Lauren, the only friend she'd allowed to see her true existence—and had no one to call on if she needed help. Her stomach twisted as anxiety built inside her. Her skin prickled and her heart fluttered. She shook the sensations away.

Yes, she'd be sick of her own company before long. Right now she'd love to be sharing a cup of tea with her mother, feel her father's reassuring hug. Heck, she'd even enjoy one of her father's lectures about the hazards of traveling alone. Would she one day beleaguer her children about safety? Without a doubt she would. It came with the territory, she supposed. She just hoped she'd have the opportunity to have children.

What if Dewayne found her? The memory of his last words, his voice filled with menace, echoed through her head. *"I'm coming for you, darling."* Nausea choked her. Heart pounding, she gasped for breath. *Stop it!* She sat up in bed and mentally shook herself. *Suck it up, girl. Don't let him continue to control your emotions. You got away undetected.* She plopped back down, the action shaking the van on its chassis a little. A number of scenarios ran through her mind, making her question her strength and determination. Would she have the backbone to stand up to him before he tried to kill her?

She reached down and touched the .38 Smith and Wesson on the floor beside her fold-down bed. God, she hoped so. *Hoped so? Girl, you better know so. There will be no second chance.* She didn't intend to go down without a fight this time. Even if she went to prison for killing him, being released from fear would be worth the risk.

Long ago she'd found daydreaming helped to ease her into sleep. She closed her eyes and focused on building a safe haven in her mind, one she hoped to find in her exile.

She drove into a small town somewhere in Texas or New Mexico. A nineteenth-century courthouse stood regally in the center of the town square. Families picnicked in the park across the street while others...

The sound of car doors slamming woke her. Startled, heart pounding, gasping for air, she sat up and took in her dark surroundings. *Where am I?* A ray of light from a break in the closed curtains cast a line across the floor, illuminating the shoes she'd kicked off earlier. Her van...she was in her escape vehicle...safe.

She lay back on the bed. Her breathing slowed as she listened to the activity around the trailer park. A child cried. A dog barked but stopped at a man's harsh command. *A dog. Maybe in time I'll be able to get one. It'd be good company and possibly a good alarm system.* She smiled at the picture of a hound sitting in the passenger seat of her van. Yes, it was a nice image to dwell on.

Better get a move on. She quickly rolled up the sleeping bag and stored it so it wouldn't bounce around, but she left the bed folded down. While water heated for her instant oatmeal and coffee, she checked her phone for any messages. None. Her parents wouldn't try to contact her. They knew she'd planned to leave Monday night, had been told what it would mean when she called and said she and Lauren were having a pizza party, but she'd not revealed any details. The less they knew the better. When she could, she'd contact them.

Today she planned to make it to Amarillo, Texas.

So far she'd traveled on Route 66 when she could. The Mother Road had always intrigued her, plus she hoped the less-traveled road would help her remain undetected. Dewayne wouldn't dream of her taking this path. He'd figure she'd take interstates and travel as fast as the speed limit would allow. The old road, potted and in poor repair in spots, ended completely in places, sending her to the interstate, often weaving from one side of it to the other. She wished she could travel only during the day to see more of the old highway and the vintage buildings, most crumbling skeletons of their former glory, dotting the landscape. She sighed. Maybe someday she'd have a chance.

Just after noon, she drove into Amarillo. She eyed the historic Neon Diner with longing but, fearing exposure, passed it by and opted for a large chain restaurant instead. She relaxed when she spotted several blonde women eating by themselves. She didn't want to stand out. It was best to blend in with the other diners, in case Dewayne caught her trail and asked the proprietors if they'd seen her. The frazzled waitress quickly took her order and rushed to tend to other customers. Susan sighed with relief. The woman wouldn't be able to identify her. You had to see a person to do that.

She laid a twenty on top of the check, stood, and slung the strap of her bag over her shoulder. Avoiding eye contact, she exited the restaurant and walked to the van parked near the back.

Next order of business was a little shopping. First of all for a laptop computer. She'd left her old computer at home, minus the hard drive. It added additional weight to the already heavy handbag sitting on the car seat beside her. A new purse was another item on her list.

As she drove down the historic highway, she scanned the storefronts, looking for a place where she might buy a computer. One of those supercenter places sat a block off the road, its large sign strategically placed to draw in customers, and thirty minutes later she walked out of the store with the most powerful laptop they sold and a handbag, a mid-sized shoulder bag. Her identification allowed her to pay, using her new debit card, with no problem.

She passed a trailer court, pulled into the parking lot of an economy-priced motel, and checked in. Inside her room, she brewed a cup of coffee in the little two-cup coffeemaker and sat at the desk with a cup of the hot brew and her laptop. Before anything else, she removed the hard drive and inserted the old one. Locating the files she needed to maintain her online clients, she saved them to a stick drive. Then, she typed in a government code and erased the drive. She removed the old drive and set it aside to toss later, along with the wig.

With the new hardware in place, she set up the email account. A message popped up on the screen.

You've got mail.

She opened her account and, sure enough, she had one message. It was from Lauren. *Why had she emailed?* They'd agreed not to get in touch for a month or so.

She clicked on the message.

Dear Shannon,

I have kept something from you, so please forgive me. I have terminal cancer of the liver. I didn't tell you before, as I knew you'd alter your plans, and I couldn't allow you to do that. Your friendship has been dear to me. If you hear of my sudden demise, don't fret over the circumstances. It was my choice. Hopefully, my way out of this world will have erased your problem.

Be happy.

Chapter Three

An icy chill inched up Susan's spine. She shivered and rubbed at the goose bumps covering her arms. *Not Lauren. Dear God, not my cherished friend. Please...please, God...she can't die.* She read the message again. Her *sudden demise...erased your problem....* What did Lauren mean? Sudden demise? *Calm down, Susan. Don't buy trouble. Get the facts before freaking out.*

She pulled up the *Chicago Tribune* online and searched their website for an obituary for Lauren Walker. Nothing. She breathed a sigh of relief. It was tempting to stop with the *Tribune*, but to be safe, she checked two other newspapers. She relaxed against the chair back. *Thank you, God.*

Maybe Lauren meant to warn Susan of what would come—her dying of cancer. The idea seemed surreal. She'd appeared healthy enough, but memories now flooded Susan—Lauren, who rarely took medicine, popping pills. When questioned, Lauren said the doctor gave her vitamins to take while she dieted. Her comment made sense at the time. Lauren had lost close to twenty pounds in the past two months. In Susan's opinion, Lauren took the weight thing too far. Her appearance bordered on malnutrition.

Now Susan knew why. Her friend wasn't dieting, she was deathly ill, and she'd not wanted Susan to know, to worry. Her "vitamins" were painkillers. Tears gathered in Susan's eyes. She longed to get in the van and turn the vehicle toward Chicago and be with Lauren when she passed. That's why Lauren hadn't told her about the cancer. She could be dying, but Lauren wanted Susan to survive and be happy.

She sniffed and brushed tears aside. If Lauren wanted her to live, she'd not disappoint her. She closed the laptop and, through watery eyes, stared unseeing out the window at the few cars in the parking lot below. It'd be several hours before guests started checking into the motel.

The urge to speak to Lauren gripped her. She returned to the chair and struggled to resist picking up the cell phone on the desk beside the laptop. She fisted her hands and put them in her lap. They'd agreed to wait six months before making contact. Hopefully Dewayne would give up the chase by then.

Susan snorted. If the idiot possessed a lick of sense, he'd give up after a month, but his hate and a mean streak drove him. He might never stop searching. Six months was too long. Lauren might not live that long. What was she thinking? Liver cancer patients rarely lived three months, much less six.

A sob swelled into a wail. She stumbled from the chair and fell across the king-sized bed, curled into a ball, and let her sobs consume her. She pounded the bed and buried her face in the pillow. *Her friend, her dear friend...dying.* Life wasn't fair. Why couldn't the cancer victim be Dewayne? Lauren never hurt anyone, always helped others. She didn't deserve to have her life cut short. Dewayne cared for no one but himself. Rotten to the depths of his soul, he did nothing but deliver pain and heartache. Again she wondered what had happened to him to alter his personality so. He'd always been selfish, but not cruel.

Dewayne had wooed her with expensive dates, flowers, candy, and gifts. Her parents hadn't approved of him but tried to keep from nagging her with their concerns. She'd been swept off her feet, thought he was the ideal man. When he proposed, she'd readily accepted. Early in their marriage, he'd been good to her. They'd been content, if not deliriously happy. They'd been married less than a year when reality set in for Susan, and she realized Dewayne lacked the most important qualities needed in a good husband— patience, loyalty, strength of character, and dependability. Dewayne cared for her, she knew that, but he cared more about his needs and concerns than he did hers. Then he'd fallen in with Leo Sharp. The drugs and then the violence began. If she'd been a little older than her twenty-one years, had listened more to her parents, insisted on a long engagement... But she hadn't.

Her swollen and gritty eyes grew heavy. She closed them. A nap would help her body. Nothing could soothe her. Sometime during the night she kicked off her shoes and crawled under the covers fully dressed.

****

"You're a lucky man, Dewayne." The doctor, who had to be at least eighty years old, removed a pair of glasses from his black bag and then snapped the case closed. Though the doctor had removed the bandages from Dewayne's eyes the previous day, his vision was still blurry. "These glasses will help you see clearly."

Dewayne took the black frames, held them close to

examine them. Damned things would horrify anyone with a sense of style, him included. He snorted, but carefully put them on. The thick lenses sat heavy on his nose. The doctor's face came into focus. Ah, better. He could perceive every wrinkle, pit, and wild hair on the old man's ancient face.

The doctor picked up his bag and started for the door.

"I'll eventually be able to trash these, right, Doctor?"

He stopped and turned back. "I'm afraid not. Sorry. Be grateful you're not completely blind."

As the doctor closed the door, Dewayne picked up the mirror lying on the bedside table and studied his profile. The glasses were damned ugly, but he could deal with them. The condition of his face was another story. The blaze had singed his eyelashes and eyebrows off and left his skin blistered and blotchy. Hell. He looked like a freak. One more thing to chalk up to Susan. The bitch had burned him again in more ways than one.

He snorted and picked up the remote control. He eased back against the pillows, and flipped on the television. A local female newscaster stood in front of a burned house. It was Susan's. He leaned forward and turned up the volume.

"Investigators announced early today the blaze at Susan Lawton's home was intentionally set. Authorities aren't revealing details but said someone set the fire from within. The body found in the ruins is believed to be Miss Lawton. Speculation is that she committed suicide. We'll keep you—"

Dewayne clicked off the set and tossed the control

on the table. *Set from inside... No shit... The bitch killed herself and tried to take me with her.*

****

Carson held his hand open, palm up. His Uncle Buck peered down at the tiny object. At just after six a.m., they stood behind the counter of the restaurant, waiting for customers to come in. "I swear to God, Carson, I wasn't at your place last night." He winked and nodded at Aunt Leona. "Your aunt had me otherwise engaged."

Carson shook his head. "Whoa! Too much information."

Leona swatted Buck on the butt. "You old goat. The windows rattled with your snoring by nine o'clock."

Well, that little bit of information cleared Buck of being his visitor. It had been after eleven when he'd turned in last night.

Leona grabbed Carson's hand. "Let me take a look at that." Her glasses hung from a ribbon around her neck. She slipped the skinny lenses onto the middle of her nose and bent in close to get a good look. She gasped and jumped back. "Could this fetish be one of Grandpop's?" She leaned in again, picked the raven up, and held it between her forefinger and thumb, turning it nearer the light. "This carving appears to be very old and fine. This bird has an inlaid turquoise eye, but many of the newer ones have other ornamentation." She shrugged. "Not that I'm trained in Zuni art, but I wonder if it could be from Grandpop's missing collection. Threw Dad into a tizzy when he couldn't find them. Evidently he didn't know about them until Grandpop was on his death bed and talking out of his head. Dad almost tore this place apart, searching."

Buck crossed himself. "Hell, son. Old Riley's ghost visited you last night."

Carson, knowing "Old Riley" was the local nickname for his great-grandfather, stifled a laugh at his uncle's expression. His aunt and uncle believed in ghosts and such. Not that he didn't believe, because he did, but he'd never heard of spirits moving objects around. Of course, he hadn't studied the subject, either.

Leona shivered. "Just be glad he didn't show himself to you. I bet he'd be a scary apparition. I've not seen *him,* mind you, but I did catch sight of a phantom when we camped down in Chaco Canyon as a child. Dad told me I must have the special gene. I had nightmares for months after."

He knew she meant the hereditary trait that allowed some people to connect with spirits. The characteristic had skipped his mother, but not him. Gramps had been with him the first time Carson had seen one of the ghosts. His grandfather assured him there was nothing to fear. Easier said than done, for a nine-year-old. "Where did Grandpop get his collection? If the figures are as valuable as you suspect, how'd he come up with the money?"

Aunt Leona handed the raven back to Carson. "You know Grandpop was full Laguna. He married a woman from the Zuni Pueblo. We've always believed the collection was hers." She patted his hand and nodded toward their table. "Come, sit down, and let's talk."

"All I know is Lily Riley, my grandmother, died shortly after Daddy was born in 1931," Leona began. "Your mother and I weren't close to Grandpop and didn't spend much time with him in the years before he died. We were more interested in young men." She sighed. "So we wasted a lot of time we could have spent learning about our grandmother and Grandpop's history. I suppose Daddy knew all the facts, but it just never came up."

Buck came over with a mug and a pot of coffee. He refilled their cups, filled his own, and sat down. "You might find something in the storage shed. Surely there are old family papers, albums, or something out there that might be of use."

Leona tapped the table with her knuckles. "That's right. I remember Daddy going through Grandpop's stuff, boxing it up, and putting it in the storage shed. We did the same with some of Daddy's stuff." She stood and bustled into the small office to the side of the kitchen. Within a minute she returned with a key ring. "Here you go."

Carson shoved his chair back and stood. He took the key and stuffed it into his jeans pocket. "Thanks, Aunt Leona." He kissed her cheek. "When I get time, I'll go through everything and hopefully find a lead."

The door of the café opened, and their first customer of the morning came through the door with a flurry of cold air. A young woman whipped off a knit hat and stuffed it into her coat pocket. With her fingers she fluffed the chin-length blond strands of her hair.

Hans, with tail whisking back and forth on the rug, studied the newcomer with interest. He sat up on his haunches and chuffed in hopes of gaining her attention.

She smiled at the dog. "Well, hello there. Are you guarding the door?" She leaned down and patted his head but avoided looking around the room. She moved to the table closest to the door, removed her coat, and slipped the garment over the back of the chair.

Hans started to follow, hoping for more attention.

Carson snapped his fingers. "Hans. Stay." Hans plunked his butt back down.

Carson placed a menu and a glass of water in front of the lady. "Can I get you a cup of coffee?"

Smile timid, she glanced up for a mere second, long enough for him to glimpse robin's-egg-blue eyes, clear fair skin, and pink lips free of makeup.

"Yes, thank you. And a glass of orange juice." She kept her head slightly lowered. Her hair draped forward, covering her face.

"Coming right up." Too bad. The woman was too pretty to be so shy, or maybe insecure. He wondered if she lived in the area.

He carried both beverages back to her table and took her order. The door opened and several people came in, halting any questions he might have about where she hailed from. By the time Buck called, "Order up," the room was half full.

****

Susan enjoyed the buzz of voices in the small café. Warm inside, its activity of patrons and workers alike soothed her, but she tensed every time the door opened, afraid she'd been caught. If those who entered glanced her way, they nodded and moved farther into the room. Many knew each other and threw comments and teasing taunts back and forth.

When the door burst open with a whack, hitting the wall behind it and rattling the small window, Susan froze and watched from the corner of her eye as two men came through the doorway. Dressed in biker gear, one of the two hooted and charged the man who'd served her. He caught him in a bear hug. "I couldn't believe my ears when I heard the news. Had to check it out for myself." He set his captive on his feet, looped his elbow around his neck, and dusted his head with his knuckles. "It's about time you came home, buddy."

The man twisted out of the biker's grasp and pounded him on the back. "It's good to see you too, Joe. Sit down and have some breakfast. I should get a break here in a minute, and we can catch up."

Joe pulled off his leather jacket to reveal a sleeveless T-shirt exposing bulging arms covered with tattoos. He yelled into the kitchen. "Hey, Buck. Leona. Glad to have your nephew home?"

A petite older lady waltzed from the kitchen carrying a pot of coffee. "Of course we are." She poured a cup of the brew for him and one for his companion. "I guess that means we'll be seeing more of you now." She yanked on his ear. "You better not be getting our boy into any mischief."

"Ouch, Leona! You can't blame all those incidents on me. Carson hatched as many plans as I did."

Carson, huh? Nice name.

Leona sniffed and propped a hand on her hip. "Well, I've forgiven you for talking him into joining the Army."

The topic of their conversation joined them. "Now, Aunt Leona, I've told you a thousand times Joe didn't have a thing to do with my decision."

She reached for his head, and he slapped his hands over his ears, saying, "We're entirely too old for your correction."

An older man in the kitchen cackled and yelled,

"Son, your aunt will stop telling you what to do when she's dead, and not a minute before."

Evidently everyone in the room knew these people and appreciated the byplay between Carson, his friend, and his aunt and uncle.

Enjoying their banter, Susan hid her smile and waited for her meal. Customers passed the biker's table and greeted him with enthusiasm. She wished she lived a normal life and could be part of such a community.

From the glowing neon sign out front to the vintage red Formica-and-chrome tables to the old photographs on the wall, the place fit her image of dining along Route 66 in the 1950s. It'd be nice to walk around and closely study the pictures. Maybe another day, when she wasn't running from Dewayne.

"Here we go."

She started as the large-framed man set her food in front of her and refilled her coffee cup. When had he gotten up from the table with his friends? She glanced to where he'd been sitting. The two men eyed them with interest, big grins on their faces. The biggest one, Joe, winked at her. She ducked her head. This was entirely too much attention. Just what she didn't need.

"Cut into those eggs and see if we got them right."

She picked up a wedge of toast and poked the yolk with the pointed end. They were cooked just as she liked them, with the white done but the yolk still runny.

"They're perfect."

"Good. Can I get you anything else? Ketchup? Hot sauce?" The warm depth and timbre of his voice washed over her body like a soothing balm. She wondered if the enticing resonance matched the man himself.

"No. Thank you." She chanced a sideways glance at him. Her heart thumped as she reached for her coffee cup. It rattled against the saucer. She caught it before it spilled. No one else seemed to notice. She chanced another peek. Of medium height, with dark hair and eyes the color of chocolate, he studied her intently, a smile tilting the corners of his mouth. Was he flirting with her? Flustered, she returned her gaze to her food and fumbled to unroll her napkin. Her silverware rattled as she grasped her fork.

"Hey, Carson." A woman at a far table spoke over the low hum of voices. "Turn on the television, will you?"

He moved to the corner of the room and turned on the set placed high enough for the entire room to see. A weatherman graced the screen. From the colors and arrows on the U.S. map, it appeared the weather would be cold but not freezing today in the Albuquerque area. The same wasn't true for the northern states, which were in for some arctic temperatures.

She finished her meal while listening to the national news in the background. Nothing she hadn't heard before. The DOW was down, oil prices increased, extreme weather conditions, and another pro athlete had been caught using drugs to enhance his performance. She rummaged through her purse for her wallet and removed a twenty. When she glanced at the television again, a reporter stood in front of a house fire.

"Authorities think the explosion...home destroyed by fire...believe the body...that of Susan Lawton..."

Susan couldn't breathe. *Fire? Her home destroyed? Body?*

Chapter Four

What the hell...

The attractive woman rushed out the door like the cops were on her tail. She'd not even put on her coat but had simply thrown it over her arm. Carson strode to the window and peered out. Her camper van threw gravel as she sped out of the parking lot.

He watched her head west on Route 66. *Hope she knows the road ends in about a mile.* Something had spooked her. He glanced at the television, trying to remember what stories had been broadcast. Darn. He'd wanted to find out if she lived around Siesta. *Oh, well, too late now.*

****

The cold night air nipped at Carson's ears as he stood under the stars waiting for Hans to finish his business. He stretched to ease the ache in his back. With the police force, he'd experienced both physical and mental fatigue. Working on your feet all day resulted in a different kind of tiredness, not necessarily good, either. Standing in one place was a lot harder than moving around. Plus, it wasn't doing what he loved. Not that he hated it, but police work was his life, and he doubted he'd ever be content to stay here and work. But he'd promised Aunt Leona he'd give her and Uncle Buck some time off. Maybe he'd be able to work through his demons while doing so.

He glanced around the courtyard, pleased at the glow of lights in windows and the occasional sound of a guest's voice. All but the first cabin were occupied. Aunt Leona had said, twice, "Don't fill number one unless you absolutely have to. The ghost lives in there, and he doesn't like just anybody bunking with him." She said people had been known to leave in a hurry in the middle of the night.

Carson grinned. He'd spend some time in the cabin when he got the chance, put the spirit rumors to rest. He sighed. The raven turning up still bothered him. He didn't want to believe a ghost had waltzed into his cabin and left it on his table. That was hard to buy, but how else could it have gotten there?

Unfortunately, he and Aunt Leona hadn't had a chance to talk further today about Grandpop's fetish collection. Carson was curious to learn more about his great-grandmother's Zuni heritage. It made sense she would be the original owner of the collection, but why hadn't it gone back to her people rather than to his great-grandfather? Well, why should it? If the fetishes of the collection were hers, then they'd go to Grandpop and then to Gramps.

Hans stopped searching for the perfect spot and, with ears tilted forward, alerted on something in the darkness. He whined, trotted back, and nudged Carson's leg. Obviously, whatever the dog sensed wasn't dangerous, or he'd be growling. Carson peered into the inky expanse west of them. Not an occupied building for a mile, but a faint glow in the approximate area of the abandoned travel court down Route 66 was visible. That motel sat back from the old road and had been vacant for at least twenty years, probably thirty.

Carson studied the light. Maybe headlights reflected off some object, but the glow didn't waver. Surely someone wasn't camping out in the overgrown trailer court there? A fire, if not controlled, would spread rapidly in this dry winter weather. He didn't know who owned the property or he'd call and report his suspicions. Hans whined again. *Hell. Guess I'll have to check things out.*

"Okay, boy—" Before he could finish, the dog took off through the scrub brush. Carson yelled, "Be careful."

He rushed inside and grabbed his revolver and a large flashlight. *Dammit! Just what I need—a little exercise to ease my aching back.* He jogged through the thick weeds, tripped on a rock, and almost fell. *Damnation. Watch your feet. If you step in a hole you'll be lying out here in the cold until morning.*

****

Susan stifled her sobs, sucked in a lungful of air, and choked. She coughed and wheezed, trying to catch her breath. It took several minutes to regain control of her breathing. For a minute there she feared she might choke to death out here in the middle of nowhere. Wouldn't Dewayne get a kick out of that? She swiped at her tears of exertion. At least the spasm had been a distraction. She'd spent the day alternating between weeping and sleeping, her only escape from her misery. Lauren was dead, and Susan's poor parents thought the body in the fire was Susan. Did she dare try to contact them and ease their minds? If she did, would Dewayne somehow be able to trace the call? She didn't know what to do.

When she left the diner this morning, she'd been

intent on getting away. Her friend had been killed in an explosion and fire in Susan's own home. It was her fault. If Lauren hadn't been aiding Susan in her escape, she'd be alive today. The horror was too much to process. Susan had driven down Route 66 until the road dead-ended. Sitting back from the road on her left sat an abandoned travel court—alone and neglected. The large ramshackle café next to the road hid much of the parking area. Overgrown with weeds, the small areas of asphalt were broken and uneven. She'd pulled around behind the restaurant and parked close to the building. Between the restaurant and the cottages, she remained hidden.

Susan leaned back in the chaise lounge chair she'd brought along for just this purpose. Of course, she'd pictured an RV park, or possibly a campground at a state or national park. Tired of being cooped up in the van, she'd come outside to do her mourning, and to think and plan. A Coleman lantern cast enough light for her to see for several yards into the surrounding night. Her .38 lay in her lap under the blanket. She sighed. It was time to put her grief behind her and move on. Lauren had sacrificed herself to give Susan more time. Thinking Susan was dead, Dewayne would give up the search. After what her friend had given, she had to be successful in her escape, else Lauren's early demise would be in vain. Lauren's death gave her one more reason to hate Dewayne. He'd caused the explosion and the fire. Of that she was certain.

Her camping spot faced the dilapidated travel court rooms. They were connected by small garages. At one time they'd been the height of fashion as far as motels went. Now they resembled skeletons of a time gone by.

The once-graveled parking area hosted weeds and grasses. Trash blown in on the wind littered the area. Fortunately, the spot where she'd parked was less overgrown, and she'd deemed it safe to place the lantern several feet from the foot of the recliner so she wouldn't be lit from behind.

The sky above her resembled an endless length of dark blue velvet whose uneven surface gave it shades and textures. Stars dotted the expanse, and a few twinkled. She closed her eyes and pulled the blanket up around her shoulders. The air, though crisp, smelled clean and refreshing. It was peaceful here. If only things were different—if she were in a different place in her life, not on the run and hiding from Dewayne.

Yet, if that were the case, would she be out here in the middle of nowhere? Alone? For all she knew, she wasn't by herself. Anyone could be out there beyond the lamplight. Her skin prickled. Should she get in the van and head farther west? She peered into the darkness, looking for signs of danger. Nothing. Nothing she could see. She closed her hand around her gun. Its presence lessened her apprehension somewhat. Her eyes burned, and she allowed them to drift shut...for just a minute.

Few sounds permeated the darkness. The muted road noises and the hum of tires on concrete from Interstate 40 resembled the drone of insects, the occasional eighteen-wheeler louder in its insistent thrum.

Something wet and cold touched her cheek. She slapped it away, as her eyes jerked open and a screech ripped from her throat. She scrambled from the chair, revolver clutched in her hand. With the gun held in front of her, she turned, searching for…for what…what…a wolf? She screamed, "Get away. Shoo." She cocked the gun, and trained it on the beast. No, it was a dog. The animal started toward her and then stopped, plunked its butt down not far from her, tilted his head, and woofed as if he wanted to play.

She giggled, and then sobered when the shepherd's ears perked and he turned toward the east. The sound of running footsteps crunching on gravel drew her attention away from the animal. Startled, she turned and aimed.

"Drop your weapon, lady, or I'll shoot." The voice from the darkness belonged to a man. "The dog won't hurt you."

Susan struggled to keep her voice steady. "You drop…your gun…first." The hand holding her gun shook so hard she had to steady it with her left.

The man stepped into the circle of light. "Look, lady, the dog is mine. He won't hurt you, and neither will I. He heard something and thought you were in trouble. Took off before I could stop him." He smiled and patted his leg with his free hand. "Come, Hans." The dog trotted to his side.

Hans? Wasn't that the name of the dog at the café this morning? The man—the one who'd served her breakfast?

His eyes darted around her makeshift campsite. He raised an eyebrow. "Looks like he might be right. You shouldn't be out here all by yourself. You have car trouble?"

Heat rose in her face, and Susan prayed he couldn't see her flush of discomfort in the glow of the lantern. She could imagine how odd her being out here alone appeared. "No."

When she didn't elaborate, he sputtered, "What the hell are you doing out here, then?"

"I received bad news today, the passing of a dear friend. I was too upset to drive. Not that it's any of your business."

He ignored her rudeness. "Oh, I'm sorry, but hey, you can park your van at the motel up the road. There's no need for you to be out here all alone." He tucked his gun in his jacket pocket, stepped forward, and offered his hand.

"Carson Rhodes. I own the Siesta Motel and Café, where you stopped this morning."

She studied him a moment, then made up her mind. She transferred her gun to her left hand and, with her right, shook his. "Su...Shannon Langley." He remembered her from this morning? Darn! That wasn't good. Probably his buddies did too. She didn't want anyone to be able to identify her. But what did she expect after making goo-goo eyes at him? She'd better be more careful.

"Where are you headed?"

She said the first thing that came to her mind. "Santa Fe." *Oops, that's not good.* Santa Fe was east of Siesta. But, this man didn't know she was from the other side of Chicago.

"Strange time of year to be taking a vacation." He shrugged. "Not that this area isn't beautiful all year round, but most tourists come during the summer." He raised a brow, a habit she supposed. "Unless they're here to ski."

"No, not hardly. I'm on sabbatical from my job and using the time to tour New Mexico. I've always been interested in the Indian pueblos, and summer is too hot to go traipsing through ruins." Man, she was getting good at lying.

His eyes narrowed in thought, as if trying to make up his mind whether she was telling the truth. He said, "Come over to my place. You can plug into the electrical, if you want. No charge."

It was tempting. She didn't feel secure in this isolated location, but getting close to this man might be more dangerous than staying here. There was something about him... His presence was reassuring, but still he had an air about him that spelled danger. Not a physical threat, but one of discovery. Just a single person learning her identity could set Dewayne on her trail. Plus, why was he being so nice to her?

"No, but thank you. I'm just fine, so take your dog and go."

He crossed his arms over his chest. "Sorry. Can't do that."

"Why the heck not?"

"Couldn't live with myself if I left you out here all by yourself and something happened. We don't have much crime, but it never hurts to be careful."

She looked around at the darkness beyond the halo of light. The cottages that had appeared non-threatening when she'd driven in now cast ghostly shadows. It was quiet but for the sound of faraway traffic. A few lights twinkled in the distance. No, she didn't feel particularly safe, but she wouldn't let him know. "I've got a gun."

"Yeah, I can see that. Can you shoot someone if you have to?"

Hell if I know. No, I take that back. If Dewayne stood here threatening me, I'd have no qualms about firing. "Yes."

"What if an intruder caught you unaware and you didn't have time to use your weapon? Unless you've practiced often, you're at risk, a possible victim."

She adjusted her grip on the revolver pointed toward the ground and squinted to peer into the shadows. Could someone be out there? His comments didn't reassure her, but she'd made up her mind. Locked in the van with her gun, she'd be fine.

"If you don't come with us, Hans and I will sleep out here on the cold ground. I'm not leaving you out here alone."

The stubborn man. Why did he care? He didn't know her. She studied him closely. He wasn't anything like Dewayne. This man's good looks weren't polished but rugged, his facial features chiseled, not pretty. His stance, though relaxed at the moment, implied power and agility. He'd not been winded from his run when he arrived, either. She didn't doubt he could move with deadly speed if he chose to. How she knew he wasn't a threat to her, she didn't have a clue. There was an air about him that radiated integrity. Susan resisted the urge to snort. Like her instincts were trustworthy. She'd married Dewayne, and look how that turned out.

Though he wore a warm jacket, she didn't want to think of him sitting out in the cold all night. She glanced down at his dog. His heavy coat would keep him warm. Her gaze returned to Mr. Rhodes. "All right. I'll drive back with you to the motel." She'd leave early in the morning, before she had to face him again.

"Good. I'm glad that's settled."

Chapter Five

It was five a.m., still dark out. Showered, shaved, and dressed for work, Carson looked out the window. No lights could be seen in Shannon's van. He grinned. He'd expected her to skip out before he got up so she wouldn't have to face him this morning. Something wasn't right about her situation. His police officer instincts told him she'd lied to him about where she was going and why. He'd bet she was on the run, but from what? From the law? He hoped not. A husband, boyfriend? That thought didn't sit well with him, either.

You're disgusting, old man. She's not from around here and won't stay. Even if she did, she wouldn't be interested in him. Oh, he knew women liked him well enough. Janet, his ex, had certainly pursued him with a vengeance. They'd been happy until she got tired of the odd hours and of him leaving her alone too much when a case needed his attention.

He'd had plenty of women friends in Albuquerque, but they'd been merely friends, someone to spend time with, have sex with. Shannon wasn't the type. This woman signified home and family, and she was young—probably too young for him.

Thirty minutes later he stepped out the door of the café, Hans on his heels. He walked over to Shannon's van and knocked on the sliding door. Rustling could be heard in the rear of the vehicle.

A sleepy voice asked, "Yes, who is it?"

"Carson. The coffee is ready. Breakfast in five minutes."

"Oh, I'm fine, but thank you."

"Aunt Leona is waiting to meet you." Grinning, he added, "She's already set a place for you at the table." She'd been full of questions about their late-night guest and horrified to hear where he'd found Shannon.

He chuckled at the small tad of irritation in her voice. "Oh, all right. You go ahead."

"No, I'll wait."

Five minutes later, she opened the door. The wind caught her hair, brushing it across her face. She'd left off her coat and hat. Her sky-blue turtleneck sweater hugged her curves and smoothed over shapely hips, her legs encased in worn denim jeans. His pulse raced in appreciation. *Down, Carson. She's leaving after breakfast, and you'll never see her again.* If he could get her to open up, to tell him what kind of trouble haunted her, he might be able to help her. If she'd let him.

****

Filled with trepidation, Susan stepped from the van. Carson Rhodes was too nice, and she feared he saw too much. Eating breakfast with him wasn't a good idea, but he'd gone out of the way for her last night. Accepting his invitation was the polite thing to do. Then she'd head out. She hoped she didn't regret accepting his hospitality.

She took the hand he offered. Her heart thrummed with pleasure at his friendly smile. Close-cropped dark hair emphasized brown eyes. Form-fitting jeans and a black T-shirt revealed muscled biceps and taut abs.

How could the man be in such good shape and work in a café? Maybe he jogged or worked out every day.

They entered the restaurant through the back door. A woman's laugh tinkled over the bass of a man's mumble, both against the backdrop of clanging dishes and silverware. The aroma of fresh coffee and bacon filled the air. Her mouth watered in response.

"Here we are, guys." At the sound of Carson's voice, the sounds stopped. A short Native American woman, wrapped in a too-large white cook apron, looked up. A smile lit her face as she approached. It was his aunt, the woman who'd teased him and his friend the morning before.

"Aunt Leona, this is Shannon Langley." Carson gestured toward the redheaded man at the table. "And that is Uncle Buck." The older man grinned and waved.

Leona took her hand and led her to a table. "Hello, Shannon. We're pleased to have you join us for breakfast."

Shannon. Would Susan ever get used to her new name? She'd tried to make it as close to her own as possible, but it still fell foreign on her ears.

Buck lurched up and pulled a chair back for her. "Have a seat, Miss Langley. Your pretty face will brighten up our breakfast considerably."

Carson snorted. "Watch out for the old coot, Shannon. He's a flirt. I don't know why Aunt Leona puts up with him."

"Because I'm a wonderful lover, young man, that's why."

"Buck!" Leona set a plate of biscuits on the table and thumped him on the head with her fingers. "Behave. She's not used to your outrageous behavior."

Shannon giggled at the horsing around between the three.

Like yesterday, the food was good, the company better. She needed time with other people; she'd been alone for too long. It must be nice to have a close-knit family to joke with, one that would hold up under considerable teasing. Susan enjoyed listening to them. She gathered from the conversation that Leona and Buck would be leaving soon. Carson had just returned, from where they didn't say, and he'd be running the café and motel with the help of a few hired people. He needed to hire two more.

Customers began filing in, and Susan rose to leave. Leona pulled her aside, her brow furrowed. "I don't know what's going on in your life, child, but if you need a safe haven, you'll find it here." She patted Shannon's hand. "Remember my words."

Voice too choked at the kindness to speak, Susan nodded.

The older woman smiled and then turned toward the counter and started serving coffee.

Carson took Shannon's arm and escorted her out the back door. She wondered why his touch evoked warm sensations in her belly when that of all other men, since her divorce from Dewayne, caused fear and revulsion.

He stopped at the driver's side of her van and opened the door. "No more camping out in isolated spots, all right?"

"Okay." She grasped for something to say, to prolong this moment. She liked this man, but she had to go. "Thank you for last night and the breakfast."

"You're welcome. Be careful." He turned and

walked back inside.

****

Susan stared into the flames of her campfire. She'd left Siesta almost a week ago. After backtracking to Santa Fe and Madrid, New Mexico, she'd turned west again and ended up at the campground in Chaco Canyon. She'd toured the ruins of several Anasazi pueblos. A book she'd purchased in the visitor's center fed her imagination about the life of these pueblo people. Fascinating! She loved history, and this was an area she knew little about. Relaxing in her lounge chair and sipping coffee, she let her mind conjure up visions of ancient people going about their evening chores a thousand years ago. She could see women bending over their cooking pots while the men tilled the crops that had once grown plentifully due to irrigation and rainfall running off the canyon walls. Children's laughter rang across the canyon floor as they ran and chased each other in games. Tonight the pueblos were mere shells of their former glory. Did the spirits of their people visit in darkness, mourning the loss of their past way of life?

At one time they'd been prosperous, trading turquoise for needed supplies. Several theories abounded as to the cause of their extinction. Some rumored they became cannibalistic. Susan preferred to believe they'd left the area and blended with the other pueblo Indian tribes in the area—the Hopi, Laguna, Acoma, Zuni, and others.

On occasion she'd felt the presence of their spirits. Goose bumps had peppered her arms and almost driven her inside her van. She'd persevered and allowed the haunting atmosphere to wash over her. Tonight the tall canyon walls surrounded her like a lover's arms, peaceful and calm. She sighed. If only the spirits could make decisions for her.

She needed to make up her mind what to do—whether to settle or to keep running. Could she stay in a place like Siesta and remain undiscovered? Maybe, but probably not. Carson appeared to be an intuitive man, trustworthy, one who would protect anyone who needed him. Leona's words rang in her ears. "If you need a safe haven..."

What if Dewayne found her and hurt Carson or his family? Was settling for awhile worth putting them in jeopardy? She didn't know what to do.

She gazed into the fire, its movement hypnotic, while she swallowed her comforting brew. The soft sound of foot drums accompanied by a flute reached her ears. Now how did she know what foot drums sounded like? Oh yes, from the CD she'd purchased at the gift shop. She glanced toward her van. Had she left the disk player on? No. She'd turned it off just before stepping outside. Hair rose on the back of her neck. She looked around expecting to find reenactment dancers approaching. No one was in sight. She listened. Was it her imagination? No. The sound echoed clearly on the slight breeze.

As a child she'd seen spirits or ghosts that appeared at odd times and places. Though their presence had frightened her, they hadn't been threatening. Eventually she'd accepted their company as normal. Then during her early teens, they'd left her alone.

As the beat grew in volume, the flames in the campfire separated to form dancing warriors. One warrior broke away from the group and stalked toward her, a lance held in his hand. The lone feather decorating his hair danced in the wind. His dark eyes held her transfixed as he grew closer, becoming more life-sized with each step. When he stood before her, she leaned back in her chair to distance herself, too afraid to try to stand and run.

He shook the lance. His voice, low and guttural, called, "Trust, daughter."

Susan jumped as the warrior disappeared, his shape pulling apart into nothingness. A crow cawed on the canyon top above. Her eyes returned to the fire and then back to the canyon wall. The crow called again.

****

Damn the probation officer and damn Susan—the bitch! May she forever burn in hell. She'd disfigured him, and now he was on the run.

His probation officer had taken one look at his burned face and reached for the phone. Dewayne knew the game was up. Before the man could pick up the receiver, Dewayne popped him in the face and took off at a run. He'd barely made it out of the building as officers dove to catch him. A block away, he lost them in the foot traffic on the street. He was wanted in connection with the explosion and fire. Susan had set him up, sure as shit.

Thank God he'd stashed a wad of money and could pay cash for the cheesy motel he checked into. The place didn't have surveillance cameras. He'd be safer here than at the local four-star inn.

He yanked the ugly red floral bedspread off the bed and flung it into a corner. He'd seen that television show about dirty hotels. He sure as hell didn't want to wallow in someone else's semen. Fully dressed, he stretched out on the sheet covering the lumpy mattress.

It sagged on the side next to the night table, threatening to dump him on the floor. The spotty carpet didn't look inviting. No telling what had been spilled on it over the years. Someone had dropped a hot iron, leaving a permanent imprint. With the TV remote in his hand, he scooted to the center of the bed and stuffed both pillows behind his head.

The news blared from the set's speakers. He froze. *Damn.* His mug, without the scars, of course, splashed all over the screen on Fox News. "Dewayne Holt, recently released from the Illinois State Prison, is wanted by authorities for questioning...explosion and fire...believed to be headed to Ohio..."

His chuckle turned into a rip-roaring laugh. *Fooled you. I'm in Kansas, dickheads.* Of course, they thought he'd head straight for his brother's. What kind of fool did they take him for?

"Body found in the blaze is not that of Susan Lawton." His laughter died, and he turned up the volume. "At this time the remains of a woman between thirty and thirty-five years old have not been identified, but they do not match Miss Lawton's most recent medical records. Sources say extensive dental and plastic surgery was required after the last vicious attack by her ex-husband, Dewayne Holt. Miss Lawton is wanted for questioning..."

"Son of a bitch!" He hurled the remote at the far wall. It shattered, and parts fell to the floor and slid behind the television set. A loud pounding from the room next door bounced the picture on the wall. He flew off the bed to retaliate but stilled as the announcer said, "Fire investigators say the trigger that caused the blaze was set from within and was a deliberate act."

"Well, no shit. Took you experts a week to figure that out?"

He paced the room, restraining the urge to hit the walls, to break something. It wouldn't do to have someone knocking on the door, remembering his scarred face.

So, Susan was alive. He snickered. His naive little wife had developed claws. Guess she'd finally grown some backbone, too. Good. Nothing worse than a whipped-down woman. He didn't want her cringing in a corner when he caught up with her.

They'd once been a happy couple. Then he'd gone into debt and gotten involved with Leo and his illegal activities. Dewayne enjoyed the money, the drugs, and the women. Susan rode his ass, cried, and threatened to leave him. No woman walked out on him. Marriage was forever. His mama had drilled her Bible teachings into him. When he'd finally had enough of Susan's whining, he hit her to shut her up. She'd gone to the police, and then the feds. The last time he'd hit her, he'd meant to kill her.

The drugs fed a wickedness inside him to the point that he lost control. He'd enjoyed hurting her—and screwing her—as she begged him to stop. He shuddered at the memory of her tight little body and how much fun it would be to break her again. One last time.

****

Shannon pulled into a fast-food place in Grants, New Mexico. Few cars surrounded the place. It was after dinnertime, and her stomach growled loudly enough to be heard over the radio. It wasn't her favorite burger place, but they had good salads. Plus, she'd be able to use their free wireless internet service. She'd not been online the entire week of camping in Chaco Canyon. The area was too isolated for cellular service. She needed an update on the explosion and fire.

Susan carried her tray to a booth in a less crowded section. Anxious to check the news, she started eating while her laptop booted. She'd bookmarked the Chicago newspapers and scanned the articles in each one until she found what she looked for—the identity of the body in her house. *Body found in fire not that of Susan Lawton.* Shannon breathed a sigh of relief. Thank God her parents now knew for a fact she wasn't dead. *The identity of the individual is yet unknown. The body is of a woman thirty to thirty-five years of age. Actual cause of death will be determined after an autopsy is performed. Authorities are asking Susan Lawton to come forward to answer questions. The fire was intentionally set from within the home. Her ex-husband has been identified as a person of interest. Just released from...*

The fire was set from within? Susan shivered in revulsion. Had Dewayne somehow gotten inside and killed Lauren before setting the fire that caused the explosion? Her stomach lurched at the horror Lauren must have experienced. Dammit. Why didn't she get out of the house like they'd planned? Had Dewayne set the fire after killing Lauren, or had Lauren rigged the house to blow up? Susan might never know.

****

Carson, on his way to bed, paused when a vehicle stopped outside his cottage. *Shit. Can't you read the No Vacancy sign?* He was dead tired but stepped back into his shoes and started for the door. Hans waited, his eyes following Carson's every movement. Someone knocked.

He opened the door.

Shannon Langley stood outside, her expression hesitant, as if she struggled to decide whether to stay or run.

Carson resisted the urge to whoop. It wouldn't do to scare her away. Plus, being so glad to see her wasn't necessarily a good thing. It'd be too easy for him to become attached to this woman.

She looked great, her hair loose and brushing her cheek. She worried her bottom lip with her teeth. "I'm sorry to stop by so late."

"It's not a problem." He stepped back. "Come in."

"No, but thank you." She looked back toward the road. "I see you have a No Vacancy sign, but I wondered if I could park my van here again." Head tilted, she grinned and leaned down to scratch Hans's neck. "I thought about the abandoned motel but feared Hans would rat on me."

"Got that right, huh, boy?"

The dog woofed and his tail beat a blissful rhythm on the carpet.

"You need electricity?"

"Yes, please, but this time I insist on paying." She removed her wallet from the purse hanging from her shoulder.

"You can pay on one condition."

Her smile wilted and brow furrowed. "What condition?"

"You'll come in for breakfast in the morning."

"You've got a deal."

Chapter Six

Susan didn't know exactly what had prompted her to return to Siesta. Was it Leona's encouraging words? Or those of the Indian warrior? She snorted. Not likely. Lordy, she must've been drugged, to have imagined the dancers in her campfire and hear the music. Maybe somehow she'd sampled a tad of peyote. *Yeah, like it dropped from the heavens into my cup of coffee.* No, more likely the stress of her situation caused her imagination to run wild.

She hopped out of bed and turned the thermostat up to sixty-eight degrees, then hunkered back down in her sleeping bag to wait for the van to warm up. It was decision time. She needed an excuse to stay here, one that wouldn't arouse suspicion. Health leave? That was an idea. She'd pretend to be getting her strength back from some illness. A specific disease would have to wait, as nothing in particular came to mind. Hopefully he wouldn't quiz her.

Maybe he'd need a website designed for the motel and restaurant? If he couldn't afford her services, she could always work for camper hookup and meals. She'd have a place to stay for a month or so and would have time to explore the area, too.

The café was in full swing when Susan entered. Hans woofed in welcome. Carson carried plates to tables but glanced up and flashed a smile. Her lips twitched in response.

Leona bustled over and hugged her. "I'm so glad you came back, child."

"Thank you, Leona. This is such a friendly place I couldn't resist returning and getting to know the people and the area better."

She didn't fool the older woman. One eyebrow rose a notch, but she smiled. "Good, good. Have a seat over there." Patting Susan's shoulder, Leona eased Susan in the direction of a table at the back of the room. "Carson will be with you in a minute. Want some coffee?"

"I'd love a cup."

Susan hung her purse on the back of her chair and sat down, scanning the room. She noticed several people studying her with interest. For some reason their perusal didn't scare her. Maybe it was the family atmosphere in the place. From the conversations and comments back and forth between tables, most everyone knew each other. One person in particular— an attractive, thirtyish woman moving among the tables and refilling cups—eyed Shannon intently. She wore tight jeans and a T-shirt that emphasized smallish breasts that jiggled freely as she moved about the room. When the brunette caught Susan scrutinizing her, Susan smiled at her and broke eye contact. So, it appeared Carson had found a waitress.

A cup of coffee appeared on the table in front of her. "Good morning." She glanced up as Carson set another cup across from her. "Know what you want to eat?"

A few minutes later he returned with two plates of food and sat down with a sigh. "Man, I needed a break.

Food service is tiring work."

Susan could imagine, what with standing all day. When she looked up from her plate, she caught Carson studying her. Heat rose to her cheeks. She resisted the urge to cover the faint scars on her face. The surgeon had assured her they looked like nothing more than age lines.

"You look good this morning—rested."

She relaxed. Yeah, she'd slept well. Making a decision helped. "Thank you. I did sleep well." She grinned. "I guess having Hans nearby for protection eased my mind."

He clapped his hand to his chest and laughed. Shannon's heart thumped at the sound—and stopped all together at the dimples that appeared in his cheeks.

"I'm sorely wounded that you doubt my ability to defend and protect damsels in distress."

She giggled. A first for her in several weeks. Her humor vanished. She didn't want anyone to be responsible for her care, to go against Dewayne if he came for her.

"Shannon?"

She stiffened and met his eyes.

"Are you running from someone? Someone trying to hurt you—an abusive husband or boyfriend?" Yes, the man was intuitive, maybe too much so for her to stay here.

"No, what makes you think that?"

"The expression on your face."

"Oh, that. I was remembering something from my past."

His furrowed brow indicated he wasn't convinced.

"Really. I'm on health leave from my job and plan

to tour this area."

"So, we might see more of you around here?"

"More coffee, honey?" The new waitress appeared between them with a pot in her hand.

Shannon wasn't sure who the "honey" was directed to, but the woman never took her eyes off Carson. Her expression resembled a cat about to enjoy a bowl of cream. Shannon watched Carson to see if he encouraged her interest. She bristled at the blatant sexual suggestiveness of the other woman. Surely Carson could see through her machinations and realize her intent. Was she staking a claim?

"Yes, Gina, thanks." He raised a brow in question in Susan's direction, and she nodded. "Fill both our cups."

"You're welcome, honey." She leaned forward and poured, her breasts on a level with Carson's eyes. When Shannon caught him looking, his face reddened.

Smile of satisfaction on her face, the waitress filled Shannon's cup and moved away to other customers.

Shannon couldn't resist asking, "She wasn't here the other day. Is she new?"

"Yeah. I'd hoped you'd come back and take the job."

"Me?" Shannon looked around the room. She could do it, if she had to, but to maintain her image of being on health leave, she'd be safer not to appear to need work. "I appreciate the thought, but I wouldn't want to take a job from one of the locals. Plus, I'm on paid leave, so I don't need the money."

"Ah, a woman of leisure."

"Well, no, I wouldn't say that. I'm still working on several accounts. I design websites in my spare time." It hadn't been her main career path, as she'd worked as a programmer until she resigned several months ago from the large firm where she'd worked for the past eight years. Her web design business was small, but she hoped to expand and obtain more clients in the near future.

He sat up straighter. "Really? Would you consider creating one for me? I'd like to bring in more business."

"Sure." This was working out perfectly. "How about we trade services? Free hookups and meals for three weeks in exchange for the website."

His eyes narrowed, brow furrowed. He sat back and folded his arms across his chest. "Nope, can't do that."

Oh, shoot. She'd asked for too much, or maybe he couldn't afford losing that much income.

"How about we trade for room and board? You must get tired of being cramped up in your camper van. You can stay in cabin number one."

She'd love getting out of the van for awhile, being able to stretch her legs.

"Of course, you'll have to share with the resident ghost."

"You're kidding, right?"

"Afraid not. Word is, guests leave in the middle of the night. Can't get out of here fast enough."

From her childhood experiences, she believed ghosts existed, but she hadn't seen one in years. Her experience in Chaco Canyon had unnerved her somewhat. She wasn't about to share that little tidbit, though. No, what she'd seen in her campfire was the result of stress and grief. Not a ghost.

"If you're afraid, we can do the hookups."

"The ghost and I will get along just fine." It'd be nice having a real bathroom, a convenience she had missed the last couple of weeks on the road. She'd develop a great website for Carson and, when her three weeks were up, decide what she wanted to do—settle here or move on.

****

Dewayne cringed as Leo Sharp's grating laugh echoed through his cell phone. "The lady rigged an extension cord to spark when the door opened."

What lady? Who was fool enough to blow themselves up for a friend? Surely Susan hadn't murdered the woman. Nah, she wasn't capable of hurting an animal, much less a human being. She'd always been a sap. "Has the body been identified yet?"

The voice sobered. "Nope. Has the cops stumped. No one's reported a woman missing. Her DNA isn't in the system. It was a well-hatched plan, that's for sure."

Yeah, she'd outsmarted him for now, but that would change. He'd find the bitch.

"How you doin', Dewayne, son? Face healed? Doc said you'd carry some ugly scars for the rest of your life." He snickered.

Dewayne cleared his throat. "Exactly. I look like a freak." Yeah, it was another mark against his ex, and it was mighty unkind of Leo to rub his disfigurement in. *Sorry shit!*

"Well, I'll have a job for you soon. Save some of that hostility for the mark I have for you."

Dewayne shuddered. It was one thing to murder someone he despised, something altogether different to kill an unknown. But he owed Leo.

"Who is it?"

"Call me in two days. I'll have the details." The phone went dead.

****

Just after noon, Susan hung the last of her few clothes in the closet. The folded ones lay neatly in the small dresser situated under the front window. Though old, cabin number one was well-maintained. The rustic wood furniture bore a patina born of constant use. Susan loved the adobe fireplace with its rough-hewn mantel. She ran a finger over one of the colorful tiles inserted below the wood shelf. The porcelain squares also adorned the curved hearth. She wondered if the geometric pattern had some meaning.

A knock sounded on the door, and Carson stuck his head in as he pushed it open. She scurried to the door to hold it for him while he negotiated a small table inside. He set it in front of the other window flanking the door.

"Will this work?" He pulled a chair over from the small dinette and slid it under her makeshift desk.

She ran her hand over the scarred but sturdy structure. "It's perfect. Thank you."

Hands stuffed in his back jeans pockets, he stood before her, eyes crinkled from his smile. Susan couldn't avoid noticing how the denim fit his muscular thighs and...other attributes. She struggled not to blush, averted her eyes, and concentrated on the fascinating dimple in his cheek.

"Good. Anything else you need, let me know." He glanced around the room. "This is the first time I've been in here in years, probably since I was a teenager."

Susan wanted to ask how many years it'd been since he was a teenager—but didn't. His age was none of her business.

62

"The place is very well maintained to be as old as it is." She didn't know for sure but assumed it had been built back in the forties, maybe the thirties.

He ran a hand appreciatively over the stucco of the fireplace. "Yeah, Granddad took over in the 1970s and worked hard to keep everything in good shape, just as his father had. Leona and Buck have kept it up, too."

"When did your great-grandfather build the motel?"

He propped a sneakered foot on the hearth and, with hip cocked, leaned forward with his forearm across his thigh. His free hand waved to encompass the room. "He built this cabin in 1930 and lived here until he finished the next. In the meantime, he made a living renting out camp spaces to travelers. The park had electricity and a bath house. When he finished number five in the 1950s, he lived there until his death. The only one Gramps built is number six, where I live."

"Are all the cabins this nice?"

"They're just as nice, but the others don't have the ornamental tile work. Great-granddaddy outdid himself on this one." He grinned. "If it weren't for the ghost, I'd trade with you."

"Ha-ha, very funny. Why do you think this is the one that's supposedly haunted? Is there something significant about it?"

"Don't have a clue." Carson chuckled. "Maybe he'll tell you one night."

Chapter Seven

Susan shoved her breakfast plate aside. If she continued to eat three meals a day in the café, she'd need to buy a new wardrobe. Well, new jeans and tops, as that's all she wore. A few pounds wouldn't hurt her, since she'd lost weight in the months preceding Dewayne's release from prison. With her stomach tied in knots, it'd been hard to force food down. She lifted her laptop and placed it on the table. While she waited for it to boot, she carried her dishes to the kitchen and placed them on the stainless steel draining area of the large sink.

Gina, draped in a full-length rubber apron, stood loading trays to slide through the industrial dishwasher. She aped a smile, her mouth a straight line.

"When you get a minute, Gina, come take a look at the pictures I snapped yesterday. Carson will be deciding which ones to use on the website."

Gina's cold shoulder warmed considerably. Her lips actually turned up a fraction at the corners. "Be there in a sec, Shannon."

Susan had no sooner slid into her chair than Carson joined her in the adjacent seat. He scooted closer and draped his left arm over the back of her chair. When he leaned in closer to see the screen, she froze. His warm scent and aftershave filled her nostrils. Butterflies fluttered in her stomach, and she struggled not to close her eyes and sniff. If she turned her head a fraction, her lips would come in contact with his cheek. Well, she'd have to stretch a little, but his tanned skin was tempting. She longed to lay her face against his for just a moment, to feel the human contact...

"Let's see what you've got."

She started and turned the screen so he could see it better. "I'll put it on slideshow."

While Carson viewed the pictures, she sipped her coffee. To keep her attention off the man, she glanced around the room. The breakfast crowd had thinned but for a few late coffee drinkers, and Hans lay on the rug by the door, napping and soaking up rays from the sun that shone through a window.

Carson marveled at the quality of Shannon's photography. She'd captured the few trees around the cabins in the pictures. In the evening shots, the two neon signs accented the lights glowing from the cabin windows, making his place resemble a small desert oasis.

"I'm impressed, Shannon. You've made these old buildings take on a new life. Are you a professional photographer?"

At his compliment, her face took on a rosy glow. "I've had a little training." She shrugged. "Took some classes in college. I've always wanted more time to pursue the art." She smiled and sat up straighter. "Lucky for me I have that now. I'm pleased you like them."

"Like? They're better than I ever expected to be able to afford."

Before he could say more, Gina dragged a chair from another table, slid close to him, and pressed a breast against his arm. "Can I see?"

He pushed back and moved the laptop over to where she could see clearly. Why did the woman have to be so blatant in her aggression? If she thought he liked her rubbing up against him, she was wrong. He glanced up to see if Shannon had observed the incident. If so, she didn't let on. Now, if it had been Shannon's breast... He jerked his eyes from Shannon's chest to his coffee cup.

Gina squealed. "Oh, I like this one. Can you put it on the site?" She turned to Carson, grabbed his bicep and squeezed. "Please." She pointed. "There's Joe and Randy. They'll be impressed to be on the Internet."

It was a picture of the waitress serving coffee to a group of the men regulars. Every morning they sat at the same table, drank coffee, and solved the world's problems. He had to admit they enjoyed Gina's banter, and she didn't back down when they ribbed her.

"What do you think, Shannon?"

He watched for any sign of dislike for Gina in Shannon's expression. Nothing. If anything, her eyes lit with humor at Gina's desire to be included in the photos selected.

Shannon leaned forward to study the photograph. "It's a good picture, artistically balanced. You might want to check with the customers to see if they mind being on your webpage."

Gina swatted his arm. "They won't care. They'll be tickled."

Carson doubted they'd mind, but he would check with the men. He swallowed a chuckle. Seeing Joe the supersized biker tickled would be fun to see. "Fine with me, then, if there is room."

Gina flounced off, a happy grin on her face. The woman did crave attention. He hoped one day she didn't invite interest from the wrong kind of man. He lifted his java to his lips and took a healthy swig.

"How'd you get her into a bra?"

He gasped, taking the coffee down in one large swallow that burned his throat. Heat rose in his face as he coughed and struggled to hide his discomfort.

Shannon grabbed napkins from the holder and handed them to him. He wiped his mouth and took a sip of water. She chuckled. "Sorry. Didn't mean to cause you to choke."

Carson waved a hand. "No problem. Your question was just unexpected." Hell, he was downright shocked at her brazen inquiry. "Uh, Leona handled the situation."

"Hmm, I don't imagine she minced words."

Suddenly, the situation struck him as hilarious. A laugh burst from his throat and echoed across the room.

People glanced their way and grinned, Gina among them, though she didn't appear pleased. Surely the woman didn't know the subject of their humor. No, she hadn't been near enough to overhear.

"No...no, she didn't." He leaned in and whispered, "Told her if she wanted to see tits flopping around, she'd go to the barn and observe the cows. Said to either put on a bra or don't come back."

Shannon giggled, and Carson knew his smile grew with each chuckle. She clapped her hand over her mouth. "We shouldn't be laughing at her expense."

He sobered. "You're right. I told Leona she'd been a bit harsh, but she insisted she'd already told Gina once. Guess she didn't like having to say it again."

Shannon closed her laptop and transferred it to the bag by her feet. "I better get to work. I'll have something for you to approve in a couple of days."

"No need to rush." No need at all. He enjoyed having this woman around. The longer she stayed, the happier he'd be.

****

Susan stretched and flopped onto her back in the queen-sized bed, kicking off the covers in the process. No matter how much she twisted and turned, she couldn't get comfortable. For some reason the cabin's thermostat wasn't working correctly tonight. It was either too hot or too cold in the little room. Earlier, she'd turned it down to sixty-eight degrees.

She got out of bed...again. Stepping into her house shoes to protect her feet from the cold tile floor, she strode toward the wall unit, flipped on the light, and checked the reading on the thermostat. *Good grief. Seventy-eight degrees!* She reread the setting. *I know I put it on sixty-eight. Now it's set ten degrees higher. Am I going nuts?* She slid the control back down.

Something wasn't right, but she didn't know what. A sound, one she couldn't identify, like possibly water running in the toilet or wind whistling through a window—but she'd checked both. She slowly swiveled, checking the dark corners of the room as she did so. Nothing. Not a blooming thing out of the ordinary. She chuckled. Nary a ghost. Darn Carson's hide for putting that ghost bug in her head. She switched off the light.

Shuffling to the bed, she kicked off her slippers and crawled between the covers. She lay still and waited for the heat to click off. And waited. *Darned if it didn't feel even hotter.*

She hit the mattress with both fists and then sat up and screeched. "All right. I've had enough. If you're Mr. Riley's ghost trying to make yourself known, then stop playing games and show yourself. I'm not afraid of you." *Liar. Goodness, please don't.* She might claim to be unafraid, but she'd not seen a ghost since childhood, and back then her perception was different. Then there was that image in the flames at Chaco Canyon, but she'd chalked that up to a vivid imagination and the mystifying air surrounding the Anasazi pueblos. "If you want to, that is, but please leave the heat alone. I'll end up with a cold."

Still nothing, and the heat continued to blast. If it didn't stop soon, she'd be opening windows. "Don't you know ghosts usually cause cold spots, not hot?" She shrugged a shoulder. "Not that I'm an expert, you understand, but that's what they say on those TV shows where they hunt ghosts, and in the books I've read. Plus, the ones that visited me as a child didn't ever try to roast me. What kind of spook are you, if you don't follow the rules?"

Suddenly the heat clicked off. She raised her eyes to the ceiling. "Thank you, God." She probably sounded like a total idiot, but... "And thank you, Mr. Riley."

Susan caught a faint whiff of pipe tobacco. It wasn't unpleasant, yet smelling smoke made her uncomfortable. "Don't be setting any fires in here. Carson would kick me out." The odor disappeared.

Odd. She shivered. The room grew cold. She lay down, settling her head against the pillows, and pulled the covers up to her chin.

"Are you still here?"

The heat clicked on and then off. Her heart thumped in her chest, and goose bumps dotted her skin. "O...kay, I take that as a yes. Can you show yourself?"

In front of the fireplace, a faint glowing vapor morphed into the shape of a man wearing a loose-fitting long-sleeved shirt tucked into buckskin-type pants held up with a multi-colored woven belt. Calf-high moccasins matched his pants. His blurred facial features morphed into angled planes lined with age. No doubt he'd been handsome in his prime. Long, silver-streaked hair, held by a headband, flowed around his shoulders. Below a broad forehead with prominent brow bones, dark eyes studied her. Why, he greatly resembled the Indian who had appeared in her campfire in Chaco Canyon. Surely it couldn't be the same man.

Susan couldn't breathe. *Calm down. If he planned to hurt you, he'd have done it by now, right?* Her breathing calmed and the knot of fear in her throat lessened. "Sh...should I be afraid of you?"

A muted chuckle reached her ears. "No. I mean you no harm." His voice, a soft guttural whisper, set her nerves on end.

Shit, shit, shit. Susan drew the covers over her head and, body shaking like she had the ague, snuggled down into the bed as far as she could. A ghost was in her room...had spoken to her. Oh, Lordy, Lordy, I can't believe I actually asked for this.

When her trembling subsided, she peeked out from under the covers. Her eyes, fully adjusted to the dark, peered into the far recesses of the room for any sign of her visitor.

Nothing. No one was there—if there ever had been. Was she losing her mind? Had the stress and fear of fleeing from Dewayne unhinged her? She didn't feel any different than she had the day before.

Maybe she'd dreamed the entire experience.

Chapter Eight

Carson turned the small porcupine fetish toward the sunlight to better examine it. "And you found it where?"

"On my bedside table this morning." She threw up her hands and sighed. "You probably think I'm crazy, but I swear it's not mine." Hands steepled atop the table, she added, "Not that I wouldn't love to own it, but for some reason I think it must be valuable."

He'd listened to her describe her heat problem during the night. Leona and Buck had never mentioned complaints from former guests about the heat. Their gripes involved thumps, scraping chairs, and the smell of tobacco. Could his great-grandfather's ghost really be haunting cabin number one? Or not just Shannon's cabin but possibly the entire motel? After all, he'd had a guest, too.

He cleared his throat. "I received a fetish the night I arrived. Aunt Leona swore it was part of Grandpop's collection, which hasn't been seen since before his death."

"Really?" Her blue eyes widened. "Then I'm not crazy?" She leaned back in her chair and blew out a breath of air. "Whew. I was worried I'd gone nuts."

He set the fetish on the table.

With a finger, she moved it around to face her. "It's a porcupine, right?"

"Yes. It represents faith and trust." He touched the turquoise arrowhead attached with sinew wrapped around the porcupine's body. "Was there anything else on the table?"

"Just some kind of gold powder. I raked it into the trash can." Her eyes rounded. "It wasn't gold dust, was it?"

He chuckled. "No, it was cornmeal, food for the fetish's journey. Actually, true fetishes are carvings that have been blessed. Otherwise it would just be a piece of art."

"How do you know so much about these little figures?"

"When I was ten years old, Gramps took me to a museum in Albuquerque that held a large display of both Zuni and Navajo fetishes. I was fascinated, so much so that I spent a month's allowance on a book about them. Gramps and I pored over the book many a night." Now Carson knew why the older man was so interested. He wondered why Gramps had never mentioned Grandpop's fetish collection. Did he know where it was hidden? If so, why hadn't he told someone?

She smiled, the expression easing the worry lines around her mouth. As if remembering last night's visitor, her smile wilted. "Do you believe in ghosts, spirits?"

"Yes, I do. It's part of my Laguna heritage, plus I accept as true all phenomena in this world until it's disproven."

"So, you think your relative is sending me a message?"

"Who knows? It's possible. If there really is a

treasure hidden somewhere, he's leaving us clues—the raven for mystery and the porcupine for trust and faith. Not much to go on."

"Why on earth would he leave me hints? I'm not part of the family. He doesn't know me."

Carson wondered the same thing. Who knew how these things worked? "I don't know. Maybe he feels connected to you somehow, senses he can communicate with you." *Or perhaps he feels her insecurity and is offering assurance.*

Eyes round, her mouth dropped open. "Me... Uh, I can't imagine why." She snapped her mouth closed and worried her bottom lip.

"Are you sure? Have you never seen or felt anything supernatural before?"

She picked up the fetish, placed it in her hand, and ran a finger across the rough edges. "Maybe. I'm not sure."

****

After breakfast, Susan found herself in the front seat of Carson's truck, Hans in the back seat. Carson had insisted she make the trip to Zuni Pueblo with him. Though the Navajo and Hopi also made fetishes, Carson believed the ones carefully packed in cotton in her purse were Zuni. His knowledge about the tiny pieces of artwork fascinated her. She admired his interest in his heritage, and his knowledge. All she knew about herself was that her distant ancestors hailed from Europe.

"How were you able to get away from the café today?" She'd been telling him about her ghost experience, and before she knew it, they were headed west on I-40.

"Called Aunt Leona and explained the situation. She told me to leave and not worry about the café."

"I thought they'd leave on their vacation today."

"Nope, not until next week." He turned toward her, a big grin on his face. "Uncle Buck wants to vacation at home. Aunt Leona's not having it. She said she's going to Nashville next week whether he goes or not."

"She's something else." Susan admired the older woman. Leona had spunk. What would it be like to have such a secure relationship that you could make a comment like that to your spouse and not fear retribution? Would she ever know? She knew many marriages were happy and not abusive. Dewayne hadn't always been explosive. His personality change occurred slowly. The drugs and then his greed had made him crazy.

She shuddered. Stop thinking about the past, Susan. "Do you think he'll go?"

"If he knows what's good for him, he will." He snickered. "Actually, Buck's resistance is only to aggravate her. He wouldn't even let her drive to Albuquerque without him."

"You mean he's possessive?"

"No, not at all. They've been together so long he wouldn't know what to do without her around."

That was nice. Her parents were pretty much the same way. Oh, Mom went on day trips with girl friends, and her dad went on a weekend hunting trip once a year, but that was pretty much the only time they were apart. Nostalgia welled up inside her. She longed to see her parents, to lean into her mother's embrace and weep against her shoulder. She missed talking to Lauren. Tears threatened, and she breathed deep to keep them at bay.

"We're about to turn off the interstate. How about a restroom break?"

She coughed into her hand to ease the congestion in her voice. "Sounds good." A diversion was just what she needed to take her mind off her maudlin thoughts.

Inside, the truck stop resembled a small city. It housed a restaurant, small deli, shower facilities, and cubicle-sized rooms for sleeping. Everything a trucker might need lined the walls and shelves of the store— even children's toys and bouquets of flowers for the wife or sweetheart.

When Susan exited the ladies' room, Carson looked up from a newspaper and dropped it back onto the stack. "How about we go ahead and eat? There won't be many places to stop from here on."

Susan let her eyes drop to the exposed front page— the *Chicago Tribune Herald*—her heart in her throat. She quickly scanned the headlines she could read while standing, and then released the air she'd held in her lungs.

Carson studied her, brow furrowed. "Would you like a newspaper?"

"No. Why do you ask?" *Liar.* She did want one but couldn't find an excuse to buy one.

"The way you stared, I thought you wanted to read the Chicago news. Do you have family there?"

She shook her head and hoped he didn't think her nuts. She waved her hand. "I just had one of those déjà vu...whatever... moments. You ever had one of those?"

"Uh, as a matter of fact, I have." Hand at her back, he steered her in the direction of the restaurant. "Now, it's time for food. I'm starved."

****

A bell tinkled above the door as they stepped into the showroom of Paul Zeekya's shop. A few customers bent over glass showcases, waited on by an older man and a young woman. The two shopkeepers smiled in welcome before returning to their patrons. Carson and Shannon peered into cases, admiring Mr. Zeekya's work.

"You are Carson, Leona's nephew?"

Carson looked up and shook the older man's hand, shocked the man knew his name.

"Yes I am. How'd you know?"

The ancient artisan chortled. The expression emphasized the wrinkles in the weathered skin of his face. Though he was dressed in jeans and a plaid flannel shirt, his shoulder-length hair was held in place with a wide woven headband. "Your aunt called to tell me to expect you."

Carson turned to Shannon. "This is Shannon Langley."

"Hello, Miss Langley."

"Mr. Zeekya."

"I'm pleased to meet you both."

Aunt Leona hadn't mentioned she knew this Mr. Zeekya, had just given Carson the name and address of his shop. He'd ask her how she knew the man as soon as he had the chance.

"Thank you for seeing us today on such short notice."

"I'm pleased you've come. Follow me." Using a cane for support, his back bent, he shuffled toward a room behind the showroom. It was a large area, the same size as the shop in the front. Tools lined three walls, and a large workbench dominated the area in the center. Small hand tools covered one end, a large lamp on the other. "I'm always anxious to see exciting Native American pieces, especially fetishes."

The temperature inside the room was considerably cooler. Was it not heated? Carson glanced at Shannon to see if she felt the change. Hands in her coat pockets, neck tucked down, she shivered. He stifled the urge to put his arm around her and pull her close.

Mr. Zeekya waved at the two chairs next to the wall in the crowded room. "Pull those up and have a seat."

Carson held the chair for Shannon until she settled, then sat in the one beside her. Shannon handed him the cotton, and he carefully unrolled the bundle and placed the two fetishes on Mr. Zeekya's work table.

Mr. Zeekya flipped on the lamp, then sat and adjusted a pair of magnifying glasses over his regular lenses. He bent over the fetish he held and twisted it to different positions. After he'd examined both animals, he placed each in a tiny Ziploc bag and layered them with cotton in a small decorative box that snapped closed.

He tapped the package. "These are very fine examples of Zuni fetishes. From the way they were cut, I believe they were made before power tools were commonly used for cutting and polishing—possibly between 1900 and 1930. To verify this, they'd need to be examined by a team of experts. Very few examples remain today. Keep them safe."

Carson could only sit in stunned silence. He'd known they were valuable, but not their historical significance.

"I'd like to hear how they came to be in your possession."

Ten minutes later, after Carson and Shannon had related their ghostly experiences, the older man looked at Shannon. "He actually spoke to you?"

Shannon nodded.

He stroked his chin. "Hmmm. I'll want to hear more about this in a minute, but first..." He turned his attention to Carson. "Do you have any idea how your great-grandfather obtained his collection of fetishes?"

"Aunt Leona believes they were his wife's. Her name was Lily, but I don't know her last name. We've a bunch of boxes in the storeroom to go through, so I hope to know more soon. I do know she was from the Zuni Pueblo. My great-grandfather was from the Laguna."

"Ahh." Mr. Zeekya nodded. "I see. I hope you will examine the contents of your great-grandfather's things soon and let me know what you find, especially if you discover the last name of your great-grandmother."

"I will." Carson took Shannon's hand and squeezed. "Maybe you'll help me. You said you were interested in the Native American history around here. It'd be a great opportunity to delve into and maybe rediscover some important facts."

Her blue eyes flashed with interest. "I'd love to."

"With your permission, Mr. Rhodes, I could study our records and perhaps learn your great-grandmother's name. As you know, tribal records are important and well-documented. If they married here, there will be an entry recorded."

"Yes, I'd appreciate any help you can give me."

Mr. Zeekya nodded his approval. "Good."

Carson shook his head. "What a shame I've waited all these years to learn about my ancestry. I think my grandfather would be disappointed in me, but now that I think about it, why didn't he share his knowledge about his family with me and his two daughters?"

"Do not blame yourself. Perhaps there is a reason your grandfather didn't want you delving into his or your great-grandfather's past, some secret that had to remain hidden until a certain time."

Carson's stomach knotted. Surely there wasn't something shameful Gramps wanted to hide or cover up? Gramps was a strict man, honest and hard-working. He shook his head. No, Gramps wouldn't do anything dishonest or immoral.

"Now, Miss Langley, let's get back to your experience. Have you ever seen or felt the presence of a spirit before?"

She glanced at Carson. "Well, uh, I did often as a child, but the sightings stopped when I was around twelve." She shrugged. "I don't know why. Then, while camping in Chaco Canyon a month ago, I saw something in my campfire." Twisting her hands, she related the events of that night. Carson could only stare as the words tumbled from her mouth. Why hadn't she told him?

"You say a spirit stepped from the flames of your fire and spoke to you?" The furrows in Mr. Zeekya's wrinkled face deepened.

"Yes. The warrior shook a spear at me and said, 'Have faith. Trust.'"

Mr. Zeekya's shrewd eyes assessed her. "The spirit sensed your distress, Miss Langley. Perhaps that is why your ability to see beyond the natural has returned." He waved a finger like a windshield wiper. "Don't deny it. Anyone who looks closely can see you're hiding your emotions." He turned to Carson. "Isn't that right, young man?"

Her gaze moved from Mr. Zeekya to Carson.

Carson nodded. "I recognized it right away."

Elbow propped on the armrest of the chair, she dropped her head to her hand. "Is it evident to everyone?"

"No, just those sensitive to the emotions of others or people like me who've had special training. I used to be a police detective, and—"

She stood. "You what? I want to go!"

Before Carson could respond, she stormed from the room. What was that all about? Well, she wouldn't get far. He realized he was standing and sat back down. "I'm sorry, Mr. Zeekya."

The artisan held up his hand. "No need to apologize. I sense something evil stalking her. I don't think it is a spirit. If so, the one who showed himself in Chaco Canyon would have acted. No, the one who seeks to harm Shannon Langley is human. Watch her closely if you want to keep her safe."

A chill crept up Carson's spine. He knew it, his instincts were true. He'd recognized her unease almost immediately. "I will."

Mr. Zeekya removed a small white fetish from a drawer. He knotted a long piece of rawhide around the carving to hold it securely and then tied the ends, forming a necklace. "Give this to the young woman. Tell her to wear it at all times."

Carson pulled out his wallet.

The older man held up a hand. "No, my son, it is a

gift. It will give her the strength and knowledge she needs to bring her journey to an end."

"Thank you. I know she'll cherish White Bear and want to extend her thanks personally."

Mr. Zeekya slid the package with Grandpop's fetishes across the table. Carson took it and tucked it into his coat pocket. He didn't know what to think about today's findings. Aunt Leona knew this man, a famous artisan, and he appeared to be in tune and connected with the spirits. How else could he know of Shannon's fears? Well, Carson himself had sensed Shannon's troubled demeanor, but not the specifics.

"No thanks are needed. An evil man is stalking her. He will kill her if he can. Know this—of the things she's involved in, she's innocent, a mere victim."

"How can you know?"

Mr. Zeekya smiled. "The hows are not important. I just know. Go and protect your heart."

Chapter Nine

Protect his heart? What the hell did that mean? *As if you don't know, old man. You're sweet on the woman.* She'd become important to him. Mr. Zeekya's words spurred his determination to get Shannon to open up to him, to reveal who or what she fled from. His mind flashed back to the newspaper in the truck stop. Chicago was one clue in the puzzle; he'd bet money on the fact.

The object of his musings stood leaning against his truck, her back to him. He unlocked and opened the door for her. She slid in without a word. Once inside, he stretched the hand holding the fetish necklace out and let it dangle before her.

She stared at it. Face devoid of emotion, she said, "It's lovely," and returned her gaze to look out the passenger window.

"Take the necklace, Shannon."

Brow creased, expression suspicious, she asked, "Why?"

"Mr. Zeekya asked me to give it to you."

She took White Bear and held him up by the rawhide to examine closely. "It's beautiful." She ran a finger over the carved stone. "Look. He has a turquoise arrow attached to his back." Her eyes met his. "For safety in battle, right?"

"Yes, that's right." Her growing knowledge of

Zuni lore pleased him. "The fetish is a fine piece of Zuni art. White Bear is one of the strongest of mystical creatures. He symbolizes strength and knowledge."

"Why would Mr. Zeekya give me such a valuable piece? He doesn't even know me."

Carson started the truck. "I offered to pay for it, but he insisted the figure was a gift."

She unhooked her seat belt. "Wait. I need to go thank him."

"Mr. Zeekya said no thanks were needed. If you want, you can send him a note." As Carson put the truck in reverse and backed out of the parking area, Shannon refastened her safety restraint and then slipped the necklace over her head. He glanced down to see where White Bear nestled between her breasts. *Lucky bear.*

"Mr. Zeekya wants you to wear the necklace at all times. Never take White Bear off. He said the fetish will give you the strength and knowledge you need to bring your journey to an end."

****

Lost in thought, Susan started when Carson pulled off the road and stopped at a roadside park. "Why are we stopping?"

"I want to let Hans stretch his legs." He stepped from the cab and flipped the seat forward so the dog could jump down. "When we get back, you and I will have a talk. You're going to tell me what happened in your life to instill enough fear to cause you to flee." His handsome face wore a frown of determination. "I won't accept anything but the truth this time."

He closed the door and with long strides joined Hans, who'd located a stick, on a long stretch of grass.

The minute Carson picked it up, the dog ran long, waiting for the twig to fly through the air. Carson didn't disappoint him, and the dog caught the stick before it hit the ground. Back and forth, barking with joy and energy, Hans ran. Carson's booming laugh at the dog's antics pulled a smile from Susan—for a moment.

Her mind shifted to their upcoming talk. She resented Carson's intrusion into her privacy. Who did he think he was, to dictate to her? He had no right to expect her to bare her soul. Yes, she felt comfortable around him—liked him. Heck, what was she thinking? He made her heart race and her stomach flutter. But that didn't mean she could tell him about her past, could she?

It would be a relief if she *could* open up and reveal her deepest fears. He was a police detective, for goodness' sake. She knew she couldn't trust the FBI, because of an individual or two in their ranks. Dewayne's source in the organization might get wind and give away her location. Carson didn't appear to be a dirty cop. His family trusted him. In her opinion, that said a lot about a person. Though his days on the force were over, he probably still had connections in law enforcement. Could she trust him? Would he call one of them, find out the details of the investigation, and turn her in? For some instinctual reason, she didn't think he would. He'd keep the information to himself.

She hadn't set the fire at her house that killed Lauren. She was innocent. All she'd done was run from Dewayne and the additional pain he'd inflict if he found her. But she had set in motion the events that caused Lauren's death. A sob rose in her throat. She covered her mouth to stifle the cry that threatened to escape.

With her free hand, she clasped the bear fetish and closed her eyes. Warmth filled her hand and infused her body. A sense of well-being filled her. She sighed. Her head dropped back against the cushion of the seat. All would be well. She had to trust someone.

The driver's door opened. Shannon jumped and raised her head. Carson still wore a smile from his play with Hans. He handed her a bottle of water she assumed he'd retrieved from the bed of the truck, then set a bowl of water on the floor by the back seat, and Hans leapt up to lap at it.

Carson popped the cap on his own water. "Do you need help with yours?"

She twisted and broke the seal. "No, I've got it. Thanks."

They drank in silence for a few minutes, and then he set his drink in the cup holder. With his arm across the back of the seat, he turned to face her. He didn't say a word, just waited.

She studied the man beside her—the lean contours of his face, the expression of concern in his chocolate eyes. If she didn't confide in him, would he be angry or disgusted, reject her? She mentally shook her head. No, he wasn't the type. She drew a deep breath. The time was now or never.

"I need your promise. That you'll keep what I tell you to yourself."

"I'll not betray your confidence, Shannon. You have my word."

She drew in a deep gulp of air and let it out. "The first thing I need to tell you...my name isn't Shannon Langley. I'm Susan Lawton."

The words spilled from her like torrents of rain

from a thundercloud. This storm had been brewing for a long time. Letting the words overflow eased the pain in her heart and lifted a burden from her shoulders. Carson didn't move, didn't interrupt, and his expression of interest didn't change, so she continued. Telling him about her parents, her fear that they were worried, and her guilt over Lauren's death released the tears she'd held inside. They flowed down her face unchecked. He handed her tissues, and she wiped the moisture away and continued.

In the back seat, Hans whined in distress and nudged her with his nose. The animal's empathy increased the flow. She turned and hugged the dog. Her voice breaking, she croaked, "I'm okay, boy."

Carson unhooked her seat belt and tugged her closer to him. He wrapped both arms around her, and she wept against his shirt front.

One of his big hands cradled the side of her head against him while the other rubbed comforting circles on her back. "I knew you were in distress, sweetheart, but I had no idea how serious."

"You...you...won't t-turn me in, will you?"

"No." She felt his lips in her hair. "Never. I'll do everything in my power to help you. If Dewayne shows his face, I'll kill him and take pleasure in doing so."

"Noooo. You'd go to jail. I don't want that to...to happen. That's one reason why I left Chicago. I feared my dad would kill him and end up in prison."

"Don't worry. If I kill him it will be in your defense. After what he's done to you, no jury on earth would convict me."

She wiped her face and blew her nose. "I like to think I could kill him myself if I had to." The desire to see him dead raged in her heart. But did she have the strength to take his life? She liked to believe that if he tried to hurt her again, she could pull the trigger. She'd never know unless forced into the situation.

The safety of Carson's arms lulled her. Her eyes drifted closed, and she burrowed a little closer to the warmth of his muscled chest.

His breath rustled her hair, setting goose bumps dancing on her skin. "White Bear will give you courage when you need it. I will give you the skills needed. We'll take you to the gun range often and train. Reaction time is of vital importance. People not accustomed to going for their weapon need to practice repeatedly to shorten their response time."

Her free arm, the one that wasn't trapped between them, circled his waist. If he objected, he didn't show it as the hand at her neck tilted her head back. He kissed her forehead. She sighed and looked up at him.

His gaze, brown eyes as warm as rich coffee with swirls of caramel, burned into hers. Her breath hitched, and her lips parted.

His lips touched hers and moved carefully, invoking a long-forgotten need.

A cry rose in her throat.

He jerked back.

Struggling for air, he dropped his forehead to hers. "I'm sorry. You're not ready, are you?"

"No. Don't be sorry." She shook her head. "It's been so long since I've been kissed, since I felt the touch of another human being." She struggled not to cry as she touched his face. "I need the contact. Please, kiss—"

His head swooped down. His lips captured hers.

Warm flesh moved over hers, gently at first, then hungrily—in a dance that set her senses on alert. Her body flushed with desire and more—longing—longing for closeness with this man she trusted with her entire being. His tongue searched for entrance past her lips, and she opened, allowing him to deepen the kiss—to taste her and allow her to taste him in return. When he pulled away, her hands held fistfuls of his shirt collar.

Embarrassed, she released him and started to ease back to her side of the truck.

He stilled her.

"Stay here beside me."

The desire in his eyes reflected hers.

She nodded.

He found the center seat belt and buckled her up, then started the truck. He backed out, put the truck in drive, and headed out of the roadside park. When he hit the highway, he wrapped his right arm around her.

Susan dropped her head to his shoulder.

For the first time since leaving Chicago, her soul felt clean and free. Within minutes she was sound asleep.

Chapter Ten

Carson stopped in front of cabin number one. He glanced down at the sleeping woman nestled against his shoulder. She hadn't budged the entire trip home. She'd been carrying a heavy burden, and sharing it had been cathartic. He wished she'd told him earlier.

Hans stuck his muzzle over the seat and nudged Carson's shoulder.

"Yeah, I know we're home, boy." He didn't want to wake her. Having her at his side, even for this short time, had been nice, a sensation he could easily grow accustomed to. Arm still around Shannon—no, Susan, her name was Susan—he gently squeezed her shoulder while shaking her. "We're home."

She jerked upright and looked around. "Goodness. I slept the whole trip?"

"You needed it. Releasing all that pain and stress wore you out."

Her face flushed, and she raked her hands through her hair, attempting to put it in order. To him it looked perfect, as it always did. "I'm sorry to have troubled you with all my problems." She unhooked her safety belt and scooted across the seat.

"Wait. Don't run from me. You needed to talk, and I pushed you to open up."

"I made such a fool of myself." Back rigid, she dropped her head. "Kissing you and all."

She reached for the door handle, but he stilled her with a hand to the back of her neck. He kneaded the taut muscles. "Honey, I've wanted to kiss you from the first day I saw you." Her shoulders dropped a fraction, relaxing the tenseness in her back. "As a matter of fact, if you'll scoot back over here, I'd enjoy a goodnight kiss."

She turned, a timid smile on her face. "You're a tempting man, Carson Rhodes, but I better go in. Thank you for listening."

"You're welcome. And hey, to be on the safe side, you'll continue to be known as Shannon, even to me, until your ex is behind bars again."

She nodded.

"Don't forget to keep your bear on at all times. Even in the shower." Hell, the image of White Bear between her naked breasts made him need a shower—a cold one.

"I will."

****

Susan, deep in thought, watched the fish swim by on her screen saver. Had she done the right thing? Confiding in Carson had lifted a load off her mind and eased her heartache somewhat. Did the attraction to him spell danger of another kind—a broken heart? She'd have to be careful, guard against becoming too involved, too dependent, in case she had to run again.

Her skin warmed at the memory of his kisses. They'd been intense and caring—not designed to turn her on but to simply love her, enjoy her. She'd felt cherished in his arms. Yes, he was good—heady medicine.

She chuckled. *Get your head out of the clouds,*

Susan. She hit Enter on her laptop's keyboard, waited for the search screen to appear, and then typed in Susan Lawton. The screen flashed a page full of hits, the most current a video news clip. Susan clicked on it and waited for it to load. *Come on, come on.* Her fingers drummed against the table until the advertisement finished. She gasped when her parents appeared in the footage.

Arms around her mother, her father's voice boomed from the speakers. "...we love you, Susan. Do not contact us." His voice choked. "We're grateful to know you didn't die in that fire."

A reporter asked, "Mr. Lawton, your daughter could give detectives information on who set the fire. Don't you think that's important?"

"Of course I do. We're very sorry for the death of the woman in Susan's home, but I know my daughter did not kill her. I'll not have my child coming forward and revealing her location to that deranged ex-husband of hers."

Susan's mother pushed closer to the microphone. "I want to know why the police haven't caught Dewayne Holt and locked him in a cage where he belongs. He's the one they need to concentrate on." Mouth twisted with pain, she looked up at her husband. He patted her shoulder. "Then our baby will be able to come home."

Susan brushed tears off her cheek and chuckled. Leave it to her mother to jump to the root of the problem. Oh, how she missed them. It meant the world that they knew she lived and understood why she remained in hiding.

Two men replaced her parents in front of the mike.

The taller and skinnier of the two spoke. "I'm Detective Haney, and this is my partner Detective Williams." He turned to her parents. "Mr. and Mrs. Lawton, though we understand your concern for your daughter, we desperately need to talk with her. Miss Lawton, if you're listening, please contact us at..."

****

It had been three days since their visit to Zuni Pueblo. Carson was itching to get into the storage shed and go through Grandpop's things. Leona and Buck would leave on vacation in a few days, so he'd better get busy at it while he could find the time. He'd just finished scrubbing down the bar when Shannon strolled toward the kitchen counter, her dirty dishes in hand. "You don't have to do that. One of us will clear them for you."

"There's no need to wait on me all the time. Anyway, it's time I started paying rent. Your website is about done. I'll be uploading it to the web today. Plus the time period we discussed is about up."

Dread filled Carson. He didn't want her to leave. "You've got another week. Anyway, you're safer here where I can look out for you."

He took her hand and led her through the kitchen. "George, if you need me, I'll be out back."

"Take your time. The rush is about over."

The fresh air cooled Carson's heated skin. He glanced at Shannon and saw her shiver. Pulling her to his side, he ran his hands up and down her arms. She wrapped her arms around his waist. He breathed in her sweet scent and spoke into her hair. "I don't want you to leave."

She drew back, searching his face. "I don't plan to

leave. I just can't keep freeloading."

"You're not—"

"I know. But the website is finished. I want to start paying for the cottage and my meals. I insist."

Her expression mulish, Carson decided he'd better agree. "All right. We'll work out something. I'll give you the long-term rental rate."

"Good. Now that your site is finished, there will be very little to keep me busy. Oh, we'll have emails for reservations, and possibly some comments posted that will need responding to, but not enough to keep me busy. I'd like to do some sightseeing in the area." Her accounts would take up some time, but not enough to keep her occupied.

"I can help with that. I'd be happy to show you around, take you to places you won't find listed in that tour book of yours."

She cocked a brow. "Is that so?"

"It is. Gramps took me to places he visited as a boy where you can see ancient petroglyphs that are protected by the local tribes. Only the locals are allowed to venture onto the land. If they get special permission, that is, and I think I can get us that authorization."

"Hmm, are you trying to bribe me?"

"Could be." He traced her lip with a finger. "I might have an ulterior motive, one other than keeping you safe, that is."

"Stop that." She stiffened, grabbed his hand, and linked her fingers through his. She shot him a dirty look.

"Hey, I didn't mean what you're thinking. Get your mind out of the gutter, woman."

She relaxed against him.

"And another thing. I want you to go through Grandpop's stuff with me. Help me look for clues to his past and who the fetish collection originally belonged to."

Her face brightened. "Oh, I'd love to help you with that. I enjoy old stuff—papers, dust, digging for information." She stepped back and tugged on his arm. "Lead on to the storage shed."

Her enthusiasm was contagious. He grinned. "Let me check in with George and make sure I'm not needed for awhile. I'll grab a small heater while I'm at it. It'll be cold inside."

****

Dewayne gagged and rushed outside to the balcony. Head over the railing, he threw up into the bushes below.

God, what an awful mess. Who knew that blood and gore looked so gross? Hell, or smelled so bad? He shuddered and drew in deep gulps of fresh air. Damn, he'd better get out of here.

He stumbled back into the plush second-story bedroom, averting his eyes from the body sprawled on the king-sized bed as he did so. Leo Sharp shouldn't have any complaints. Dewayne had followed the mobster's instructions to the letter. His wife knew who'd ordered the hit on her life. She'd cussed like a sailor before Dewayne delivered the final blow that killed her—a knife to the gut. He guessed Leo didn't want to bother going through a divorce, and extracting revenge for her filing with a lawyer was a bonus.

Dewayne glanced around the room, looking for items of value to steal. He might as well make a little extra money, since he'd stuck his neck out and would soon be wanted for murder. He rifled through the jewelry box on the vanity but found only cheap pieces of junk. Shit. She probably hid the good stuff in a safe.

He stomped to the closet and shoved clothes around, leaving smears of blood as he did so, until he found what he searched for—a safe. He pulled the lever and laughed with glee. The stupid bitch didn't even lock her good stuff up.

A pair of running shoes sat on the floor underneath the clothes. He lifted a dirty sock and started filling it with jewelry. Man, old Leo had spent the bucks on the woman. He might not be too happy if Dewayne took too much. Leo probably intended to give most of it to his new honey.

Sock loaded, he jogged down the dark stairs and maneuvered his way out the back. He left the door open so the cops would think it had been unlocked. The key Leo had given him would join DeWayne's bloody clothes. The mansion backed up to a busy road that bordered the lake. He'd parked in a turnoff by a jogging trail. At his truck, he peeled off his bloody shoes and jumpsuit and stuffed them in the black trash bag, then weighted it down with several bricks from the truck bed. His latex gloves and hunting knife joined the other items. He pushed all the air from the bag and tied it in a double knot.

Yanking open the cab door, he tossed the trash bag onto the passenger floorboard. The sock landed on top, and he stepped into the shoes he'd placed just under the steering wheel. The pickup started at the first turn of the key.

Dewayne breathed a sigh of relief and pulled out

into the traffic. His debt to Leo Sharp was paid. The man better leave him alone now. He had more important things to do.

****

The child's death mask danced before his eyes. Her mother's screams bounced against his skull, back and forth, never stopping. "No, no, dear God, no..."

Something wet and cold nudged Carson's neck. Hans whined. Carson reached out and rubbed the dog's neck. "I'm okay, boy." Han's warm tongue swiped across his face.

Carson jerked up in the bed. Would the nightmares never stop? He'd give his life to bring the child back, to stifle her mother's cries of rage and grief. "Ugh. Enough." He turned to sit on the side of the bed and dropped his head into his hands, then lifted it to glance at the clock on the nightstand. It read two a.m.

He stood and strode to the refrigerator. Hans hugged his leg as Carson surveyed the shelves of the icebox. "Want a bowl of milk, boy?"

The dog gave his version of a snort and backed up.

Carson chuckled. "Didn't think so."

Without troubling himself to get a glass, Carson drank a healthy slug from the gallon container. His mother would have had a fit. She'd caught him often enough as a teenager. He still missed her. He'd been in college in Albuquerque when she died of cancer. Aunt Leona and Uncle Buck moved into her small home in Gallup to help his dad so Carson could finish out his senior year. He owed them a great debt. His father passed a year later. At least he'd died quickly, didn't suffer long. A massive heart attack killed him within seconds, or so the doctor claimed. Carson sighed and put the carton back in the refrigerator.

Back in bed, he stared up at the ceiling. *You can't change the past, Carson. You've got to deal with it and move on.* Easier said than done. Department investigators had found him innocent, not to blame for the child's death. He'd been fully exonerated. Their assurances didn't ease his conscience. If only he could put it behind him, let it go. But he couldn't. It invaded his mind at the oddest times, while working, reading a book, watching television. And then there were the times a child laughed, or one gazed up at him with innocent eyes seeing clear through his soul... He shuddered.

What would Susan think if she knew he'd killed a child? Would disgust be reflected in her eyes? Did he care what she thought or felt? *Hell, yes, I do.* More than he wanted to admit.

Tomorrow he'd convince Susan to contact the police in Chicago. He'd call Captain Farley and ask him to find out whom to contact. He'd let him know she suspected a leak in the Chicago department and in the Chicago FBI office.

No doubt about it, he was invested in Susan and her situation. He'd do everything in his power to help her and protect her from Dewayne Holt.

Chapter Eleven

Susan stared into her coffee cup, the brew as dark as the issue on her mind. Should she trust Carson's Captain Farley to keep her location secret? Problem was, the man couldn't control everyone he came in contact with, could he?

She glanced up to find Carson eyeing her. He lounged, one hip braced up against the lunch counter, arms folded across his chest. Heat from his stare warmed her. Unable to look away, she let his gaze hold hers, draw her under his spell, heating her blood as his kisses had the day they went to Zuni Pueblo.

Suddenly her mouth was dry, and she swallowed. She moistened her lips with her tongue. His gaze dropped to her lips, and she froze in mid-swipe. He smiled, and Susan prayed he couldn't see the flush that rose in her face.

She closed her mouth and smiled back just as George nudged Carson. Without looking away from her, he listened to the man. With a nod in her direction, he turned to follow George into the kitchen.

Susan watched him go, admiring the breadth of his wide shoulders and the view of his trim hips and muscular legs as he retreated from her sight. The man was beyond sexy—a temptation she longed to explore. If Dewayne knew she cared about Carson, he'd kill him just to hurt her. Though Carson could take care of himself and showed no fear of her ex, he didn't know how evil Dewayne could be. She mentally shook herself. No, she wasn't going to go down that road. Rather than dwelling on what-ifs, she'd enjoy the time she had available with Carson and his family.

They'd gone through several boxes the day before without finding anything of value to Carson's search. Carson had taken an old scrapbook filled with newspaper clippings from WWI into his cottage with him. Maybe he'd glean some helpful information from them. There were still more boxes to go through. She looked forward to checking them out. She loved sorting through old things with the possibility of finding some treasure or relic.

Right now she needed fresh air. A walk over to the abandoned motel would help her think. Hans trotted along with her. She enjoyed the dog's company but looked back wondering whether Carson cared if he left with her. He watched them leave and waved. *Guess that answers my question.*

The morning air was brisk. Susan zipped her jacket against the chill as they struck out for their destination. The wind whipped her hair around her head, and she pulled a ski cap from her pocket and slipped it on. Hands in her pockets, she followed Hans through the knee-high scrub brush, cactus, and prairie grass. Here and there rocks littered the red earth amid the foliage.

They reached the abandoned motel, and Hans rushed in and out of rooms, checking for anything living. His bark of excitement announced his success. A mouse ran out, Hans on its tail, to run between two cottages to the back and under a tall pile of brush. Hans sniffed, barked, and poked his nose into every crevice in hopes his prey would allow him to resume the chase.

Susan laughed at his antics, enjoying the sound.

"You have a good laugh."

She whirled to see Carson approaching.

"Hans is entertaining company. He's cornered a mouse."

"So I see. Hans. Quiet." Hans trotted toward him, nudged his hand and then took off again to pursue other interests. "Good boy." Carson had joined Susan atop the broken and weed-infested blacktop. "His barking can get on one's nerves after awhile."

"Yeah, but it's a shame to interrupt his fun."

He slipped his arm around her shoulders and squeezed, his embrace so natural you'd have thought he'd done it a million times a day.

Susan leaned into his side. The contact felt so right. She sighed. "I've decided you're correct. Go ahead and contact Captain Farley."

"Good." He gathered her in his arms and held her close. His warmth and strength reassured her that she'd made the right decision.

"Talking to the authorities will ease the burden of worry and fear on your shoulders."

She wrapped her arms around his waist. "I hope so, but if my location leaks to Dewayne, he'll come for me."

His hand traveled up her back and slipped under her hair to grasp her head. "I'll not let him hurt you, Susan."

She burrowed against his shoulder, enjoying the faint whiff of his aftershave stirred by the breeze. "Dewayne is evil. He'll kill you to get to me if he has to." Plus, he'd do it in such a way as to make Susan suffer more.

He tilted her head up to his and placed a warm kiss on her lips. "Trust me, sweetheart, to take care of you. In my line of work, I met many men like Dewayne and came away unscathed."

Yeah, that was true in many cases, but cops died in the line of duty all the time. She couldn't stand it if something happened to him. Oh, God, this man was quickly becoming too important to her. She didn't want to fall in love but feared she already had.

Susan leaned back to study Carson's face, searching for clues as to how he felt about her. She knew he cared, but was it just his civic duty, his desire to protect, or something more? Yes, he liked her, desired her, but...

He turned her in the direction of Siesta motel and whistled for Hans. "Come on. Let's get into town to the shooting range for some target practice."

****

Susan's ability to hit the targets pleased Carson. Now he needed to build toward a faster response time. When they went to Albuquerque, he'd see if they could use the police obstacle training range. Many individuals could shoot precisely, but being able to draw the weapon and shoot under stressful situations was something altogether different. Reaction time was of vital importance—learning to drop behind cover, stay out of the line of fire. That ability would be as important to Susan as being able to hit her target.

Her compact .38 Smith and Wesson was a good choice for her but not the greatest for concealment. He wanted her to carry something in her pocket at all times in case Dewayne caught her unaware. She needed a small semi-automatic, like a Ruger .380. They were compact and easily hidden. He'd have to determine if she had enough strength in her hands to cock the pistol.

He didn't intend to leave her alone but didn't know how to go about asking her to move into his cabin or allow him into hers. Until he could broach the subject, he'd leave Hans with her. The dog would alert her to anyone in the vicinity and protect her if need be. Carson pitied old Dewayne if Hans lit into him, as the dog wasn't known for a light touch when he came to attacking. That was the main reason Hans had been rejected from the Canine Program. The force feared he'd kill someone. In this situation, if Hans killed Dewayne, few would weep.

****

The café was unusually busy. An original establishment of the Route 66 era, the Siesta was a big draw this evening. Susan hoped her web design had captured the eye of travelers and encouraged them to stop. Tourists, two couples in their seventies and well acquainted with the Mother Road, chatted as they walked around studying the pictures. Framed clips of the Siesta Motel in its early days of construction up through its heyday in the 1960s hung on the walls, no doubt added by Carson's grandfather.

The folks sat down. One woman ran her hand lovingly over the red-and-white Formica table. "We used to have one just like this, didn't we, Henry, right down to the chrome legs?" She shook her head. "I can't believe we sold it at a garage sale." She sniffed and turned to her friends. "At the time, I thought it was ugly and wanted something new."

Henry squeezed his wife's hand. "Yep. We even

had six of these red chairs." He winked. "Those were the days, weren't they, hon?"

When the Interstate came through in the 1970s, traffic on the old road had dropped considerably. Today, Route 66 still drew a crowd as travelers of all ages wanted to capture a glimpse of days gone by on the historic road. Susan had to admit she was as curious as everyone else to see it all. Hopefully, one day she would.

****

Carson glanced up as the door opened and a tall man wearing a ski jacket entered. He carried what appeared to be a computer bag. His gaze traveled the room and settled on Shannon. He strode to the empty table beside her and sat down. Muscles tense, ready to spring into action, Carson walked toward the table, watching for a reaction from Susan out of the corner of his eye. She glanced up at the man, smiled, and then returned her gaze to the book she read.

He relaxed and stopped in front of the man's table. "What can I get you to drink?"

The stranger looked up. His face lit in a wolfish grin that set Carson's nerves on edge. This man was a predator of some kind. He'd have to watch him closely. "I'll have a coffee."

"Coming right up. I'll bring you a menu."

"No need. Just bring me a Spanish omelet with toast."

Carson strode off to turn in the order. When he returned with the coffee, the man's laptop computer sat open in the space to his left with the webcam on, Carson in full view as he walked toward the table.

"Your webcam is on."

The man smirked. "So it is."

"Turn it off." Carson tried to keep his voice civil. To soften the bite, he added, "Folks around here won't appreciate being spied upon."

He drew himself up in his chair. "Well, now, I'm not exactly spying. I just wanted to record part of my travels today, and this makes a good backdrop." He closed the laptop. "But, I'll concede to your wishes."

Satisfied, Carson left to retrieve the man's omelet and wait on several other customers. Sometime later he glanced over to see the laptop open again, webcam on. Relaxed in his chair, one ankle propped across his knee and a pencil poised over a pad balanced on one thigh, the smirk returned as his customer watched Carson approach.

Carson wanted to wipe the grin from the man's face, but tamped down his anger. It wouldn't do to make a scene in front of all these people.

He reached out and closed the computer. "I thought we'd agreed you'd not invade the privacy of these folks."

"Hmmm, that's what you decided." The man twisted his mouth and quirked an eyebrow while tapping the pencil on the notepad. "I believe it's your own privacy your trying to protect, Detective Rhodes."

Dread inched up Carson's spine. "Who are you, and what do you want?"

The man glanced around to see who watched. He'd attracted a few eyes, including Susan's. "Name is Stanley Roberts." He withdrew a card from his pocket and handed it to Carson. "Freelance reporter." He pulled a chair out and motioned to it. "Have a seat, Detective. I'd like to interview you."

Carson read the card and dropped it on the table. "I'm no longer a detective, and I'm not interested." He shoved the chair back under the table and picked up the man's empty plate. "Now get out. Consider your breakfast on the house."

"Well, now, that's mighty neighborly of you, but I'd rather pay and get a story." He stood, laid a twenty on the table, and then waved a hand as he took in the people in the room. He raised his voice. "Wouldn't you folks like to know what it feels like to have murdered a small child...in the line of duty, of course. Detective Rhodes can tell us, since that's exactly what he did while protecting the innocent in Albuquerque."

Nausea churned in Carson's stomach. He set the plate back on the table and turned toward George. The older man grinned, reached below the counter, and came up with a baseball bat. He tossed it to Carson.

Without blinking an eye, Carson caught the wooden weapon, and then slammed the bat across the man's laptop.

Stanley jumped and hollered, "Hey, you can't do that!"

Carson poised the bat to strike again. "This is my café, my property, and I said, 'Get out.' Do you need to be reminded again?"

Mr. Roberts picked up his dented computer, bag, and coat as he made for the door. At the exit, he turned. "You'll be sorry you made an enemy of me."

"Fine, I'll be sorry. Now go."

Joe, wearing a sleeveless shirt as usual, with tattoos covering his arms and neck stood and flexed his muscles. "Yeah, mister. Git. We don't like your looks. We especially don't like you digging up trash on folks around here."

Several of Joe's buddies joined him. One stomped toward Mr. Roberts and yelled, "Boo!"

Mr. Roberts bumped the door frame as he launched himself through the exit.

The crowd laughed.

"Don't pay that fool no mind." Joe squeezed Carson's shoulder. "Your friends know you didn't mean to kill that baby."

Struggling to hold himself together, Carson nodded, turned, and stalked through the kitchen and out the back door.

Chapter Twelve

Susan watched the exchange, compassion twisting her heart. He'd killed a child. Oh, God. How terrible for him. No wonder he'd given up police work. He couldn't get past the horror of it. In his shoes, she'd be eaten up with guilt. Heart in her throat, her gaze followed him as, shoulders stiff, jaw clenched, he strode from the room. She waited until everyone's attention had left Carson and then followed the path he'd taken through the kitchen.

She found him outside behind the café, arms propped, holding his weight, against the stucco building, head dropped forward. He drew in deep gulps of air. The screen door slammed behind her, no doubt alerting him to her approach. He shuddered when she touched him, but he didn't pull away when she wrapped her arms around his waist from behind and laid her head against his back. A groan rumbled from his chest. He turned, pulled her up into his embrace, and buried his face against the curve of her neck. Her feet dangled above the ground, but she didn't care. She slid her arms around his neck and held on.

Finally, he set her on her feet. She dropped her hands to his biceps. Shoulders rigid, jaw tense, a tremor shook his frame. He appeared to be ready to strike out at something at any moment. Not at her—she knew he'd not hurt her—but she feared he might bloody his hand against the wall. "I'm sorry. I relive the experience in my dreams, but I never thought to be confronted by the media again, especially way out here." He sighed and thrust his shaking fingers through his cropped hair. "I thought my nightmares would stop when the sun came up."

"I don't know all the details, Carson, just what I heard inside, but if you need someone to talk to, I'd be happy to listen."

Voice harsh, he ground out, "I don't need to talk. I did plenty of that with the department psychiatrist." He stroked her cheek. "You deserve to know what I did. I'll tell you everything later, but right now, just let me hold you." He leaned against the wall, drawing her body flush with his. With one large hand, he held her close. The other stroked her back as if each caress soothed his torment. Her heart ached for him. His heat warmed her and heightened her awareness of how right it felt to be with him.

Several minutes passed before his ragged breathing eased into a smooth pattern. He straightened and placed his hands on her shoulders. "Thank you for not condemning me. I was afraid after learning the details of why I'd left the department you'd despise me, and I'd see revulsion in your eyes."

She covered his hands with hers. "I don't know the particulars, Carson, but I can't believe you'd ever hurt anyone intentionally, especially a child." That reporter wanted to make a name for himself. In doing so, he'd be hurting Carson, painting him as negligent or, worse, criminal.

His voice hoarse, Carson uttered, "No, never." He dropped his forehead to hers. "Her mother's cries of despair will haunt me to my dying day."

"Remember this—the child's mother probably blames herself every day for putting her child in the position that caused her death. She didn't keep her safe."

His laugh bitter, he muttered, "Thanks for saying that, but I doubt it. The woman was a crack addict. Reality has no meaning to her. I'll always be to blame in her eyes."

"You must accept the truth."

He nodded, but his eyes denied his acceptance. He'd probably heard the words many times, but until he internalized them, he'd be in pain.

"I need to get back inside and help George. Think you'll be ready to go to Albuquerque day after tomorrow?"

She wasn't, but putting it off wouldn't help her situation. It'd be best to get it over with. "Yeah, I guess."

He grinned and tapped her on the nose. "That's my girl. I'll call Captain Farley and tell him to expect us."

****

Captain Farley unfolded from the chair, came around his desk, and offered his hand. "Miss Langley, I'm glad you decided to come in." He'd agreed with Carson that Susan should come in and be known under her alias and had informed the Chicago detectives to follow suit. The captain pulled a chair out for her and turned to Carson. The two men shook hands. "Good to see you, Rhodes." He nodded toward the crowd gathered around Hans outside his office. "I see the mutt is as popular as ever."

"Yeah, he's basking in the attention. He should

have been a show dog."

"Damned shame he couldn't stay on the force."

"Good for me, though." Carson glanced through the plate glass window partition. "I'd be mighty lonely without him." He turned back. "He's guarding Shannon now."

Farley grinned. "How'd you explain Miss Langley to the guys? Saw the back slaps and razzing going on out there."

"Said she was my girl friend." Susan had blushed scarlet but played along with the men's teasing comments about finding such a good looker in the backwoods around Siesta.

"Hmm, bet they enjoyed that." The old leather swivel office chair squeaked as Chief Farley sat down.

"What'd you tell them about why you're here?"

"Said you'd called me in about an old case of mine being connected to one in Illinois."

"Good cover." The chief handed him a thick folder. "Take a look at this, so we'll look legit."

Carson flipped through the folder and lifted a blank sheet of paper, handed it to the captain, and pointed to it in several places. The captain handed Carson a pen, and Carson scrawled his signature under nothing in two different spots.

Farley took the folder, stuffed the paper inside, and tossed it to a stack on his desk. His attention turned to Shannon. "Miss Langley, anything you want to tell me before I let in those two detectives from Chicago?" He peered through the privacy window at someone in the outer office. She turned to see where his gaze landed. Hands in their pockets, the two men she'd seen at the televised news conference leaned against the outer office wall, but their eyes were on her. Their posture was meant to convey relaxation, but their faces showed impatience, as did the stiff line of their backs. "If so, now would be the time."

She turned back to him. Carson laid a hand on her shoulder and squeezed, a gesture not lost on Chief Farley. He cleared his throat. "Are you sure you're not too emotionally involved here, Carson? Can you guard Miss Langley without your feelings affecting your instincts?"

Carson stiffened; Susan felt the tension in the hand on her shoulder. "I'm not on the force any longer, Farley."

The captain nodded. "All right then. Miss Langley..." He waved a hand for her to proceed.

"I don't trust the force in Chicago. Dewayne and his connections have someone on the inside. He even bragged once they had FBI associates, and I believed him. If those two detectives leak where I am, Dewayne will find me and kill me."

He stroked his chin. "Maybe we can convince them to keep your location under wraps." Brows furrowed, he thought for a moment and then turned his attention to Carson. "You need a couple of men to help out— keep watch posing as vacationers?"

"You'd do that?" Carson couldn't believe the department would help out in a case not their own.

"For a few days, a week max, just to make sure Miss Langley's whereabouts aren't leaked by her coming in today. Plus, if we caught Holt, it'd be a coup for the department. I've not revealed her identity to anyone, but you never know when a reporter might be lurking, looking for a story, or someone on the street might recognize her."

"I'd appreciate the help."

Captain Farley signaled to the two men. They straightened and strode forward.

Inside the office, Farley made the introductions. Both Detective Haney and Detective Williams were polite and thanked her for coming in. They spent several minutes going through the pretend folder and questioning Carson in front of the glass so those outside could see. Then Williams sat down where he couldn't be seen by those outside, flipped open a notebook, and waited, while Haney asked questions. "We need the name of the woman who died in your home."

"Lauren Walker."

"Why hasn't she been reported missing?"

"She didn't have family in the area. Her brother lives in Los Angeles, and they weren't close."

"Walk us through what happened on your last night at home."

Susan thought she'd been prepared for their questions about Lauren, but not for the tide of emotion that erupted as she told how she and Lauren had changed places. "But she was alive when I left. We had a car waiting for her on the road beyond the field behind my house."

"Do you think it was Miss Walker's intention all along to commit suicide?"

Voice choked, Susan said, "Yes, now I do. I realize she intended all along to take Dewayne with her. She wanted me to have a chance at life without him." Hands shaking, she wiped at her tears. "I had no idea she was sick. I knew she took pills, but she said they were vitamins the doctor gave her to help with her weight loss. She'd lost too much weight, in my opinion." Her voice trembled as she spoke. "What kind of friend can be so blind to another's health?"

Pity lined Detective William's face. "Ma'am, I suspect she went to great pains to hide her illness from you."

Haney cleared his throat and shot his partner a glare. "You said you brought your laptop with a message from Miss Walker."

"Yes." She opened the computer and brought up her emails. Williams and Haney read the message.

"May I see that?" asked Captain Farley.

They scooted the laptop around so he could see.

Haney rocked on his heels and stared down at her. "Did you have any other communication with her after you left? Anything to prove she was alive?"

For the first time since they'd entered the room she experienced fear—fear they thought she'd killed Lauren. "Isn't the email proof?"

Haney studied her. "Not necessarily. It could have been written earlier and set to be sent at a certain time."

"I did get a text message from her about an hour after I left the house. She said she was home safe."

"We'll need your phone, then, and your laptop. You can have them back after our tech guys have searched all your files."

She handed them her phone. It didn't contain any information she had to have at hand. She knew her parent's number by heart, and with Lauren gone she no longer needed hers. Her laptop was a different story. "But this is a new computer. I bought it in Missouri, and I need it for the website work I do." At least she'd backed up her files, but she hated to buy a new laptop to use until they finished with hers.

"Your old one was found in the house, but the hard drive was missing," said Haney.

"Yes, I took it with me and used a government code to erase the files. Then I tossed it into a trash dumpster in Amarillo."

One of Haney's eyebrows rose a notch.

"I used the government code where I last worked to clean drives before donating them. It's a common practice, not some big secret."

"We'll need the location of that dumpster."

She gave him the information but didn't know what good it would do, since more than a month had passed. The drive, along with the black wig she'd worn to get out of the house, was probably in some dump ground under a pile of rubbish by now.

Farley slapped his desk. "Okay, boys, do you have everything you need? Plan to charge this little lady with anything?"

"No, but we'd like for her to return to Chicago with us."

"Personally, I think she's safer here. Why don't you leave her in our custody? We'll be responsible for keeping tabs on her. And by the way, keep her location under wraps. She took a chance coming here today to meet with you. If Dewayne Holt finds out where she is, he'll try to kill her."

Both detectives stood. "We understand that, Captain. No one knows we're here today except our captain. He's as concerned as you are for her safety, especially since Holt is a suspect in the murder of a crime boss's wife."

Her gasp didn't go unnoticed.

"I imagine it was payback time for him, returning a favor," added Haney. "You have any idea for what, ma'am?"

She shook her head and stifled a shudder. "All I know is that I'm almost positive he was parked outside my house on the night I disappeared."

"Did you happen to catch the make and model of his vehicle?"

"No, just that it was an older model dark pickup."

Williams flipped his notebook closed. "Miss Langley, if it helps to ease your mind any, the coroner said Miss Walker died due to an overdose of pain pills. She was already dead when the explosion occurred."

Chapter Thirteen

"Oh, thank God." Relief washed over her features, and she muffled her cry with a fist.

Carson resisted the urge to take her in his arms and instead massaged her shoulder.

She quickly recovered, and though her voice warbled, she smiled. "I'm grateful she didn't die from the blast and fire." She reached for Williams' hand.

"Thank you, Detective. You...can-can't know how much that information eases my mind, to know Lauren didn't suffer." Her smile trembled on her lips.

The big man held her hand and patted it with his free one. "I figured it would."

Haney drew in a deep breath of air. "As much as I'd like to believe you had something to do with her death, my instincts are pretty good when judging people." His eyes met with those of Chief Farley and Carson. "I think I would recognize a consummate liar or a darn good actress by now."

"I happen to agree with your assessment, Haney." Farley, waiting by the door, shook hands with each of the men. Before opening the door, he added, "If Holt pops up around here, we'll notify you straightaway."

"We'd appreciate that." Haney turned to Carson, his eyes sizing him up. He nodded and offered his hand. "I'm sure you'll keep her safe, Rhodes. We appreciate you convincing her to talk with us."

Carson clasped the man's big paw. "You can count on it, Detective."

"Oh, one more thing," said Haney to Susan. He withdrew a piece of paper from his pocket. "I dropped by your folks' place yesterday and suggested they buy a disposable cell phone. They called a few hours later with their number." He handed her the paper. "Thought you might like to call them."

****

Dewayne spread *The Chicago Times* out on the cement picnic table, ignoring the view of the beach. Florida's April sun warmed him, so he set the box of donuts on the newspaper to keep it from blowing away and shrugged out of his jacket. He flipped open the box, removed a pastry, and swallowed it in two bites. He took a swill of coffee to wash it down, and then reached for another sugar-coated confection.

An item on the front page in the lower right-hand corner caught his attention. *Ex-con Dewayne Holt Sought in Murder of Crime Boss's Wife.* The chocolate-covered pastry hit the paper with a plop. Dewayne brushed it aside and read, his finger moving from word to word. *Investigators found Holt's DNA at the scene...* He jerked back. What the hell? He shook his head. He'd been careful. No way could they have found his DNA. He smashed the pastry with his fist. Damn it! His stomach contents. Nah, surely they didn't scrape vomit off the ground? His skin prickled. Would Leo plant evidence to convict him? Hell, yes, he would if it took the heat off of his own ass.

Dewayne grabbed up his breakfast, threw the newspaper in the trash, and with his coat folded over his arm, strode to his truck. He studied the vehicle as he approached. There wasn't anything distinguishing about the dark, older model truck, but maybe it was time to ditch this gas hog and find something else to drive. Though it wasn't showy, someone may have seen him. He'd sell it, catch a bus to the next town, and buy something there. Yeah, that sounded like a good plan.

****

The two undercover cops on loan were young, probably Susan's age. She knew looks could be deceiving and the two were capable or they wouldn't be here. Their guns tucked into the back of their jeans and probably elsewhere, hidden by flannel shirts, the two posed as a newlywed couple.

"Are you sure you know how everything works?" Susan asked as she looked around her camper van for the last time. She had mixed feelings about strangers staying in it, but Carson had assured her they'd take good care of it. After all, they'd eat their meals in the café, and she couldn't let Carson be out the expense of putting them up in one of the cabins. He'd parked it beside her cottage, putting them between her and the field in case Dewayne attempted to get to her.

"We've got it, Shannon. Not to worry. If we have problems with the heat or anything else, we'll see Carson." The pretty brunette turned Susan toward the door. "These digs are much nicer than we're used to. Now, you go about your regular routine. If Holt shows up, we don't want him to get suspicious and think this is your van."

"Right." Susan hopped out at the vehicle's side door and waved. "See you at breakfast."

She strode to her cabin to get ready for bed. Hans waited at the door. He chuffed in welcome, and she scratched his ears. "I kinda like having a roomie, boy." She unlocked the door, then turned and surveyed the vast expanse stretching behind the cottages. It'd be so easy for someone to be hiding there, but the dog hadn't alerted on anything. Her gaze returned to Hans. "Have you taken care of business, boy?" He yipped and scratched once on the door. She guessed that was a yes.

Inside, Hans scoured every corner of the room, checking for intruders. Satisfied the area was secure, he went to his bowls to see if she'd added a treat since he'd last checked. Carson had warned her Hans would con her into extra food if he could, but assured her a dog bone on occasion wouldn't hurt him. Hans cocked his head, looking at her in question.

"Oh, all right. After all, you are working. Protecting me, aren't you, boy?"

A yip answered her. She lifted a dog biscuit from the box Carson had brought over and tossed it to Hans. He caught it in midair and wolfed it down in seconds before trotting over to the rug beside the door.

She and Carson had returned from Albuquerque two days ago. No one figured Dewayne would make a move immediately if her location leaked, so Captain Farley had time to find someone to visit Siesta and help Carson. Even the best snitch system took a couple of hours, possibly a day or two, to spread the word. Plus Dewayne would need travel time. Of course, if he was in the neighborhood, that didn't bode well for her, but she doubted he had a clue she'd escaped to the west.

Her new cell phone sat on her makeshift desk beside her computer. She glanced at the time on the clock radio beside the bed. Ten p.m. Even considering the different time zone, her folks might still be up, but she didn't want to chance waking them. It'd been wonderful to talk to them again. Who'd have thought stodgy old Detective Haney could be so thoughtful as to help her connect with her parents. Susan bet her mother would keep the man supplied with baked goodies for a year.

As soon as Dewayne was caught, the elder Lawtons would be visiting Siesta to personally thank Carson, Leona, and Buck for taking their daughter under their wing. Susan settled into bed, imagining what her mother's reaction would be when she met Carson. Would she notice the attraction between them? Without a doubt she would. Her mother had already asked probing questions, most of which Shannon did her best to avoid answering. Shannon would like to have the answers herself. The appeal was there, but neither she nor Carson knew where it would lead.

Before she knew it, the week was over. Dewayne hadn't shown himself, so Captain Farley felt confident neither his department in Albuquerque nor the one in Chicago had leaked Shannon's whereabouts. He called the two officers back to Albuquerque.

Her days settled into a routine of jogging before breakfast, with Carson at her side and Hans loping ahead to blaze a trail. Then Hans would circle around behind them to make sure they weren't being followed. The dog's ability to understand Carson's commands fascinated her. She knew animals were smart, but she'd had no idea of their full potential.

After breakfast, and Carson's early shift at the café, they drove to a field outside of town where the locals had set up a shooting range. Bulldozed earth made a berm to stop stray bullets. Distances were paced off, a big board set up where patrons could staple their targets, and covered pavilions protected participants from the weather.

Carson put her through a series of exercises to increase her response time. His praise was hard won. She had to admit she'd never make a good cop, but her skills grew little by little. Hopefully she'd be prepared if she ever came face-to-face with Dewayne.

****

Frustration gnawed at Dewayne. His sources at the Chicago PD hadn't been able to ferret out any information on Susan's location from the detectives on the case. They'd learned the two had flown to Albuquerque and talked to a Captain Farley, but nothing else. Tight-lipped bastards. When he'd asked how they'd gotten his DNA at Leo's mansion, his contact had actually laughed. "You fool. Don't you know you can be traced by most body fluids?" Dewayne still heated at the memory. At least he didn't still suspect Leo for ratting him out.

Loaded down with his few grocery items, beer and sandwich makings, he stood in line, growing more impatient by the minute. Ahead of him, a little old lady, squeezed into a floral stretchy pantsuit, fumbled around in her change purse for three damn pennies. "I know they're in there." She poured the contents of the faded and cracked pocketbook onto the counter.

Dewayne rolled his eyes and turned to see if another checker was free. His eyes lit briefly on a "rag" magazine. He snorted in disgust at the headline—*Cop is a Child Murderer*. Every fool knew cops were as guilty of crimes as ordinary folks. The accompanying picture showed a dark-haired man, apron tied around his waist, hand raised in anger. A woman sat alone at a table behind him, her eyes round, mouth dropped with what he supposed was shock. Something about her... He grabbed the magazine off the rack. *Well, I'll be dammed.*

"You ready, mister?" The clerk jerked back at his grin. It was all Dewayne could do not to jump into the air, click his heels, and yell.

He straightened his face and laid his items on the counter, the rag on top. "Sure am."

After paying, he rushed to his vehicle and scanned the front page, flipped to page eight for the full story. Siesta Motel and Café in New Mexico. She might be long gone, but maybe someone would remember what she'd been driving. Hell, maybe she blabbed to one of the locals about her next destination. Not likely, but who knew? Susan would make a mistake, and he'd be there to show his love.

His belly jumped when he blurted out a hearty laugh. For some reason his body's response tickled him, and he roared with laughter. He chuckled all the way to his motel. Tomorrow he'd be on his way to Siesta. Might even take a room there and let folks become comfortable with his presence.

****

Shannon sat on the sofa in Carson's warm cabin, feet curled up beneath her, reading a book on Zuni fetishes. His cottage was slightly bigger than hers, but hers was more attractive, in her opinion. It might be due to the dark paneling that lined the walls, a decorating trend of the 1970s. Carson carried a box in and placed it on the coffee table, then sat down beside her.

He threw an arm over her shoulders, cuddled her

close, and leaned in to peer at the book. He tilted the book to see the cover. "I haven't seen this in ages. Where'd you find it?"

"On the bookshelf in your bedroom." She tapped a page. "It says here that fetishes are usually not signed, as it violates their communal purpose. So how on earth do you know who carved them?" Many were so small it would be hard to etch a name on them without disturbing their artistic image.

"Most artists believe their work is unique enough to be easily identifiable. Signing them is a modern trend initiated by tourism. Until tourism became a big part of the Zuni economy, there were very few fetish artists. Now there are close to three hundred or so."

She remembered from their earlier discussion that he'd said a carving had to be blessed before it was really a fetish. "How are they blessed?"

"The Zuni are a very religious people. The pueblos come together during the winter solstice. There, during a Zuni medicine ceremony, the fetishes are sanctified. Then they are sacred."

"Do they has less value as just carvings?"

"As pieces of art, they're of importance to their owner, but if blessed, then they're imbued with spiritual influence." Yeah, she understood that, but the idea of a little object having power boggled her mind. It was hard for her to swallow.

"I know it's hard for individuals who didn't grow up with Native American traditions to understand, but we believe fetishes aid us in a number of ways."

He flipped the pages of the book back to the beginning, where several examples of primitive carvings were displayed. "Tribal possession carvings handed down hundreds of years ago were believed to have been real animals that were petrified into stone beings."

"That's hard for the average person to believe." At least it was for her, anyway.

"Of course, but not for the Zuni. Remember, I'm talking about the ancient fetishes, those that were rectangular pieces of stone shaped into animal forms, not the commercial ones you see so many of in shops today." He tapped a picture of an early carving. If not for their names below the pictures, she wouldn't be able to identify the animals. She fingered the bear at her breasts and lifted it to study. It was easy to recognize as a white bear.

"Many blessed fetish owners have seen marvels occur in their lives—cures for cancer and other miracles that have been attributed to the spirit within the carving. And because the owner believed in the fetish's ability."

Shannon touched the bear again. "Do you think this one has been blessed?"

"Of course. Mr. Zeekya wouldn't have given it to you otherwise."

"Okay. Good."

"But you must accept its power as true."

Could she believe? No doubt she'd felt a tingle when she clasped it in her hand. She'd give it more thought. She sat up and pulled the box closer. "Let's see what's in this. Maybe today we'll find what you're looking for."

Carson removed a pocket knife and carefully slit the packing tape. He lifted the contents—several shirt boxes, a photo album filled with newspaper clippings, and a cigar box. He tossed the empty box on the floor.

Shannon rubbed her hands in glee. "I think we've hit pay dirt. There has to be something of interest here."

Thirty minutes later, they had a picture of Carson's great-grandmother and great-grandfather on their wedding day, along with their marriage certificate. Odd, they'd not been married on one of the reservations but at a justice of the peace's office in Gallup, New Mexico.

Carson held the photo. "So, Lily's maiden name was Luna."

****

Mr. Zeekya's call the next day caught Carson by surprise as he stood at the grill flipping burgers. George handed him the phone and took the spatula from his hand. "Mr. Rhodes. I've discovered your great-grandmother's name. The tribal elders would like to meet with you about your ancestor and the disappearance of a set of communal fetishes in 1930."

Shocked, Carson didn't know what to say other than, "I'll be there tomorrow." Zeekya's words echoed in Carson's mind. *The disappearance of a set of communal fetishes.* Items Carson knew were highly valued property of the tribe. No. He couldn't, he wouldn't believe any ancestor of his would steal anything, much less something of such important tribal value. There had to be another explanation. He'd try not to jump to conclusions until he heard the facts.

Shannon agreed to come with him to the Zuni reservation. For one thing, he didn't want to leave her alone at the motel, in case Holt showed up. Plus, he enjoyed having her company. Due to lack of motels in the area, they would camp in her van at an RV park in Black Rock.

Shannon reached over and squeezed his hand. "I know it sounds bad, Carson, but there could be a simple, innocent explanation. Their missing set may not be the one your great-grandfather had."

"Yeah, that's true, but not likely. A set like they're talking about is very rare. I doubt there would be two of them."

"I guess. But, you had nothing to do with it."

He knew that, but the knowledge didn't ease his distress. And if the set disappeared in 1930, why were they just now hearing about it?

Mr. Zeekya met them at his shop and rode with them, giving directions to an elder's home. Inside, a small group of men and women waited. Mr. Zeekya motioned for them to sit down and then introduced people in the room. "This is Mr. Peña. He will conduct the meeting."

Carson nodded.

The older gentleman's dark eyebrows contrasted starkly with his silver hair and deeply lined face. "Mr. Rhodes, we appreciate you coming today." He turned to Shannon. "And you, Miss Langley. We look forward to hearing about your meeting with Mr. Riley." He didn't wait for her to respond. "Now, let's get right to the point. We believe the set of fetishes you are trying to find are the ancient holy ceremonial collection that disappeared from here in 1930."

He lifted the old pottery jug on the coffee table. "This is the container in which they were housed. You're aware of why there is an opening here?" He pointed to the hole in the side of the jar.

Carson leaned forward, elbows on his knees, hands clasped. He resisted the urge to pop his knuckles. "Yes.

So they can eat when nourishment is provided."

"Ah, good. You are knowledgeable about our beliefs."

"I've done some studying on the subject. My grandfather introduced me to Zuni fetishes when I was a boy." He studied the somber faces around him. "What makes you think your set and mine are one and the same?"

The oldest woman in the room spoke up. "Because, Nephew, I saw my older sister, Lily Luna, take them before she ran away with your great-grandfather, John Riley."

Chapter Fourteen

Carson snapped his gaping mouth shut. This woman was his great-aunt. "I am honored to meet you, Aunt..."

Her ancient face crinkled, her dark eyes glistening with what Carson feared might be moisture. "Nona." She wiped a tear away from her face with the back of her hand. "I'm pleased to meet you at last."

"Why haven't we met before? I never knew I had any relatives here at Zuni Pueblo." Not that he'd asked, but his mother and Aunt Leona had never mentioned it. "Does Aunt Leona know about you? Did Gramps?"

"Your grandfather may have known, but he never inquired, so I doubt your mother or aunt knew. You see, my parents didn't approve of Lily's marriage and forbade it." She clasped her hands and leaned back against the sofa. An older man, possibly her son, put an arm around her and bent to whisper in her ear. She patted his leg and murmured, "I'm fine," before turning back to Carson.

"I was only six years old when Lily left, but I remember that day so well. My parents never believed their eldest daughter would defy their wishes. When she left, they were distraught. I didn't tell them what I saw, and it was several days before the prayer fetishes were reported missing from the church. So you see, no one knew Lily had taken them until years later. I didn't want to add to my parent's distress, so I kept quiet until recently. Now it is time for the truth to come out."

"I'm sorry for the burden that knowledge must have been all these years. Did you never try to contact my great-grandfather or try to recover them? Did you even know of Lily's death?"

Face grim, she shook her head. "No, she was dead to us from the day she left here. Her name was never spoken again."

What a loss. Here his mother and aunt had relatives they knew nothing about. Years of valued relationships lost because of something that had happened over eighty years ago. And Carson was to believe his great-grandmother was a thief? That was hard to swallow. "Do you think if she'd lived Lily would have returned the fetishes?"

"It's possible. She was angry when she took them. She may have regretted her actions later, and then died before she had a chance to return them. The key question here is did John Riley know about them, and if so, why didn't he return them? Was it spite or heartache that kept him silent?"

"I don't know, but I'll turn the motel upside down looking for answers and for the prayer set." He nodded to all in the room. "And of course, when I find them, they'll be returned to their rightful home."

****

Shannon placed two cups of water in the small microwave oven and set the timer for three minutes. When the bell sounded, she removed the mugs, added hot cocoa mix, and stirred. Carson, brow furrowed in thought, sat on the back bench seat, Hans at his feet. Since they left the reservation and driven the short distance to Black Rock, he'd said little. He'd acquired them a camping space and hooked up the utilities. They ate their sandwiches in silence, Carson deep in thought. Shannon, knowing he had a lot on his mind, let him think.

Now, with a cup in each hand, she walked the short distance toward him, careful not to spill the hot liquid. Carson took one, and she sat down beside him.

He put his free arm around her shoulders. "Thank you."

"You're welcome."

He nudged her closer and brushed his lips against her hair. His warm breath danced across her cheek. "Not just for the cocoa, but for letting me mull things over in my head."

She turned her face so her cheek would meet his lips. Hand on his leg, she squeezed. "You had a lot on your mind."

"Mmm-hmm." He nuzzled her jaw and kissed the corner of her mouth. She resisted the urge to turn and meet his lips with hers.

"Drink your cocoa before it gets cold or you spill it." She straightened and brought her cup up and took a sip. "It's already cooling down. I don't like it lukewarm."

His gaze pierced hers, his lips arched in a suggestive smile. "Neither do I."

The warmth in his look didn't refer to the beverage. Heat rose in her face and blossomed elsewhere. No, he wouldn't be a lukewarm lover. He'd expect full surrender in a relationship and give it in return. No doubt about it, this man and his sex appeal sizzled like cold water on a hot griddle. The van, which had seemed roomy enough when she'd been in it alone, grew smaller.

Easing back, he tilted his cup, taking a healthy swallow. "Well, drink up, then." He winked. "Relax, sweetheart. I can't help admiring you, but I would never take advantage of this situation."

"I know."

He peered at her over the rim of his cup. "Do you?"

"Yes. Or we wouldn't be sharing this van tonight."

He wiggled his eyebrows.

"You on the top bunk, mister." She patted the seat. "Me down here."

"Spoil sport."

An hour later, Carson's thumping and bumping on the wall in the small upper bunk woke her. At his muffled, "Dammit," she made up her mind.

She scooted as close to the back wall as she could. The bench seat folded down into a double bed, and though it would be close quarters, it'd be better than listening to him thrash around all night. They'd neither one get any sleep. "Come on down here and bring your sleeping bag."

In the filtered light, his feet and legs appeared one second before his torso slid into view. He spread his sleeping bag beside her and crawled inside. It didn't take him but a second to settle. "Thank you. I promise to be a gentleman."

Hans chuffed at being disturbed, turned around in a circle, and lay back down on the carpeted floor.

Hugging the wall, she lay with her back to him. His body radiated heat and was a temptation. *Don't go there, Susan.* She feared if she gave in to her longing for the emotional as well as the physical closeness she'd be lost. If something happened to him, or if he later cast her aside, she'd not survive. Yes, she cared entirely too much for the man. He implied he cared about her, and she trusted him with her life but wasn't sure about her heart.

His breathing evened, and Shannon sighed with relief and allowed her body to relax. His soft snore lulled her to sleep.

****

"Howdy, mister. What can I get you?" The thirtyish-something waitress averted her eyes when he looked up. Hate boiled inside. Women used to fawn over him. Now they couldn't bear to look at his scarred face. His eyes, void of lashes and brows, made him resemble one of the aliens folks talked about spotting in and around Roswell. Well, hell, the sightings were miles away.

Pasting on his nicest smile, he tried to appeal to her soft side. Most women had one. "I'll have coffee and your biggest steak with all the trimmings. Make it rare."

Picturing a big tip, he supposed, she grinned. "Coming right up." She turned in his order and returned with a mug of java. She tapped her name tag. "The name's Gina. If you need anything, just give a holler. Your food will be out in a jiff, hon."

A minute ago she couldn't stomach his ugly mug, and now she favored him with false endearments. *Bitch!* He watched her walk away, ass twitching with each step. He swallowed a disgusted snort. All women were devious.

He glanced around the room. The man in the picture, Carson Rhodes, wasn't around. It was late in the evening, past most people's dinner time. From the sign on the door, the place would close in an hour. Acting nonchalant, he took the folded gossip rag from his inside coat pocket and smoothed it out on the table.

The waitress leaned over his shoulder, purposely allowing her breast to rub against him as she refilled his cup. "My God, that's Carson." She set the carafe down, snatched up the paper, and waved it at the man in the kitchen. "George, come take a look at this."

"Do you mind?" Dewayne pretended aggravation. Inside he chortled.

"Oh, sorry. Just got excited. That's our boss."

"Really?" He bent to study the article. "Well, I'll be." He tapped the page. "Says Siesta Café right there. What a coincidence." Yeah, right.

George strode from the kitchen and put a plate in front of Dewayne. The meat covered the platter; blood ran from the beef where the pick labeled "rare" protruded from the flesh. His stomach rumbled in response to the delicious aroma. He cut a bite and popped it into his mouth, chewing slowly. "Mmm, perfect."

George nodded and turned to Gina. "Now, what are you yammering about?"

She pointed. "Look, there, at that picture."

He bent down and studied the photograph. "Damn." He straightened and shook his head. "That fool reporter. The man better hope Carson doesn't come looking for him."

Gina giggled. "Shannon looks like a doe caught in the headlights of an oncoming truck."

George stared, and muttered, "Shit." He glared at Gina. "Don't stand here yakking. Get back to work."

He stalked back to the kitchen.

Gina started to follow.

"Wait. Is this Shannon a regular here?"

Her brow furrowed. "Why are you asking?"

"No reason in particular. She reminds me of my sister." He pasted a sober expression on his face. "She died some years ago."

His sad story worked like a charm. "I'm so sorry." She glanced back at George. "She lives in one of the cabins." She winked and whispered, "I think she and Carson have the hots for each other," before starting back to the kitchen.

Dewayne struggled to keep his rage tamped down, to keep his face from reddening, his voice civil. "Is there a bar in Siesta?" He wiggled his non-existent eyebrows. "Want to grab a drink after work?"

Her face lit in a smile. "I'd love to."

George yelled from the kitchen. "Quit your gossiping, Gina. You've got work to do."

Her shoulders slumped. "Sorry, guess I better not. I have to help close, and we'll be here awhile."

****

Dewayne shone his headlights into one of the garages on the back side of the abandoned motel. Three walls would keep some of the cold at bay. The debris inside was minimal, but he didn't want to risk running over a nail and getting a flat tire. He got out and kicked boards and other trash to the corners. Back outside, he killed the lights on his car and gazed out across the field. A few lights twinkled in the distance, but they were far away. Satisfied that his car beams had gone unnoticed, he got in, backed into the small space, and killed the motor.

His watch glowed in the dark. It was almost midnight. He slid across to the passenger seat and put it in the recline position. Reaching behind him, he lifted a blanket and pillow from the back seat. Within minutes he was comfortable and warm. Fog covered the windows, blocking the outside world.

A knock on the passenger window woke him. *What the hell!*

He used the blanket to wipe the window. An old Indian man bent down and stared at him. Long gray hair held in place by a woven headband didn't prevent his hair from swinging forward. He mouthed something but Dewayne couldn't make it out, and he wasn't about to roll down the window.

Dewayne picked up the revolver from the driver's seat and pointed it at him. He cracked the window and yelled. "Get the hell out of here before I shoot."

The man threw back his head and an eerie laugh filled the car. Hair rose on the nape of Dewayne's neck. Suddenly the figure fell apart into nothingness. Terror filled him, and he choked back a howl of fright. From the confines of his car, Dewayne searched the shadows of the garage and saw nothing. He started the engine and hit the brakes to activate the brake lights. Still nothing.

Had he dreamed the entire thing?

****

Something tickled his nose. Carson glanced down to find Shannon's head on his chest, her arm thrown around his torso. Blonde hair fanned around her face, tickling his. He brushed it back, careful not to rouse her. *What a nice way to wake up.* A smile stretched his mouth, and he resisted the urge to tighten his hold on her, to turn and pull her body flush with his. *Bad idea.* If she woke, his state of arousal might send her shrieking from the bed. He stifled a chuckle and sighed. Waking up with Shannon in his arms every morning would be a welcome change in his life.

He wondered at her hesitance to take their camaraderie and mutual attraction to the next level, to have a sexual relationship. He understood her desire to keep him from becoming Dewayne's target, but he wondered if something more was involved. Had Dewayne abused her sexually, or made her feel undesirable? He couldn't see it, but people were strange creatures, and some were downright crazy. If the man had made Susan think she couldn't respond, he was a fool. Carson would have to prove to Susan that her ex was wrong.

Hans sensed he was awake. The dog yawned and stretched. He put his paws up on the side of the bed and stood on his hind legs. He stared down at Carson intently before his brown eyes flitted from him to Susan and back again.

Carson whispered, "No, boy. I didn't get lucky."

The cheeky mutt snorted as if in disgust, and then nudged Carson with his nose. Carson eased from under Shannon and rose from the bed. His jeans hung on the back of the passenger seat. He pulled off his sleep pants and tugged on his denims. As he stepped into his shoes, he glanced at Shannon. Her eyes were closed but her cheeks were pink. So, she'd peeked. He swallowed a chuckle. He hoped she liked what she saw. At least it showed she thought about his body, as the idea of what hers looked like without clothes seared his brain.

****

"Here it is, boss." Carson snatched up the gossip rag Gina slapped on the counter and scanned the page. He fisted his hands to halt the urge to slap the ridiculous grin off Gina's face. She must have recognized his fury, as her delighted expression sobered. "Sorry." Her shoulders slumped. He chided himself for being harsh. Hell, he shouldn't have remained quiet about Shannon's dilemma. He knew George was trustworthy, but he hadn't been sure of Gina. That's why he hadn't shared the information.

He skipped the image of himself and gazed at Shannon's surprised face in the background. Damn. Would Dewayne Holt likely see her, and could he be here in the area now, watching? He glanced around the room, checking faces, before flipping the paper to the front page to check the date. A week ago.

Dread twisted his gut. He glanced over at Shannon. She sat at her usual table, unaware of her possible discovery, reading the paper while she ate breakfast. Her hair brushed her cheek as she leaned forward. It had grown since she'd arrived. Soft, silky, he loved its texture against his fingers, the fragrance of her shampoo. She glanced up and smiled. He waved her over. When she reached them, he handed her the paper.

Susan peered down at the picture and gasped. The color drained from her face.

Gina wrung her hands. "Carson, I'm sorry. I don't believe what the guy wrote. I just thought it was funny to see you in the rag along with movie stars and such."

"You said a man had a copy in here last night? A customer?"

She nodded. "Yep. I got a copy at the truck stop on I-40 on the way here this morning. Had to—"

"Enough, Gina!" His mind conjured up scenarios he didn't want to consider—Shannon struggling with the deranged man, or worse yet, lying in a pool of blood. "What did this man look like?"

Her face wrinkled. "Well, he was an odd duck. Fair-headed. His eyes were cold. But let me tell you, he didn't have any eyebrows or lashes, like they'd been burned off...and his face was all mottled."

"Oh, God," moaned Susan. "It's him."

Gina whirled around. "Him who?"

"Shannon's ex-husband." He held a hand up to stop more questions from her. "Would you recognize him if you saw him again?"

"Why, sure. I bet George would too."

"Did he ask any questions?"

"Sure did. Asked if Shannon was a regular here."

Carson held his temper in check. His anger wasn't directed at Gina but at himself. He hadn't explained Susan's situation to the others to protect her privacy. He should have known better. George suspected something, though he'd not approached Carson about the matter. "What did you tell him, Gina?"

Eyes round, she glanced at George for help. His frown let her know she was on her own. "Well...I didn't think it was a secret." She bit her lip.

"Gina, hurry up. Shannon's life may be in danger."

She moaned. "Oh, God. I told him she lived in one of the cabins."

****

The sketch artist was waiting in a room outside Captain Farley's office when they arrived just after noon. By two p.m. they had a good likeness, one both Gina and George approved. Susan took a deep breath to steady herself and stepped forward. She studied the eyes. How had she not noticed years ago the hint of evil in them—evil or mental illness, she wasn't sure which. "Yes, that's Dewayne." She shook her head. Why hadn't he died in the explosion rather than coming away disfigured? His hate and desire for revenge would be even greater now. She didn't wish to see anyone die needlessly, but Dewayne was a festering sore ready to erupt. Anyone in his way would be affected.

They exited the building, took the elevator to the parking garage, and headed to Carson's truck. A few cars drove in looking for an empty space. His left arm around her shoulders, Carson's eyes scanned the area for signs of Dewayne. "You all know what he looks like now, so keep your eyes peeled."

They reached his vehicle to find his tires flat. "Shit!" He opened the rear door and shoved Susan and Gina inside. "He's around here someplace. Keep your heads down." Susan did as she was told but managed to sneak peeks through the back window.

George waved down a passing police car and, within minutes, they were hemmed in by several cruisers with lights flashing. A service crew vehicle joined them. Feeling the danger was over, Susan opened the back door and slid out, Gina on her heels. Carson observed their actions but didn't comment.

A lanky man in overalls exited the tow truck with a clipboard in hand. He eyed the tires. "Sorry, Carson. Looks like you need a full set." He bent and studied them closer. "I can't be for sure until we have them off, but it looks like a knife puncture." He scribbled on a form, ripped out the bottom copy, and handed it to Carson. "I expect your insurance will cover the replacement cost."

"Yeah, after my deductible. Can't be helped."

"I'll tow it in, get you some tires. A patrol car can bring you by to pick it up and settle the bill."

Carson handed over his keys. "Appreciate it, Frank."

"No problem. I'll call Farley when we have it ready."

A man and woman carrying evidence kits approached, with Captain Farley in the lead.

"Don't waste their time, Captain. We know who did this, and I doubt he left any prints."

"Yeah, I suspect you're right." Farley waved the team away. "Let's get you inside and order up some lunch while you wait for your truck."

Gina huddled in her chair in the corner of the tiny room, a fistful of the denim of George's jeans in her hand. For the first time, she seemed to realize Dewayne Holt meant business. Usually yakking, she didn't say a word. George stood stoically by her side, his expression one of resignation.

Susan peered over Carson's shoulder as they viewed video footage of the garage's security tapes. Within minutes they'd found him. On foot, wearing jeans, a generic black ski jacket, and a baseball cap, Dewayne turned and grinned up at the camera. Then he raised his hand in the air, middle finger up.

****

Susan sat next to Carson, cuddled against his side. His small sofa allowed just enough room for the two of them—and Hans, of course. With her feet out to the side, the big dog covered them with his body and kept her toes warm.

Carson's hand moved from her shoulder and cupped the back of her head. "I wish you'd stay here with me tonight, even though sharing the van with you the other night was torture."

"Hmm, well I have to admit, your snoring tortured my ears."

He snorted. "I don't snore! At least, I don't think so."

She chuckled. "Actually it wasn't so bad, more like a snuffling sound, like that big animal with the long snout, on that children's television show with the big yellow bird."

"You have a charming sense of humor."

"I'm glad you think so."

His strong fingers kneaded the tense muscles in her neck. She groaned and allowed her head to drop forward. He was good with his hands. The thought of him touching her elsewhere sent shivers through her frame. Oh, how she wanted to share his bed, but she couldn't. Not yet. Dewayne would kill him to get to her. She couldn't allow him to harm Carson. She needed to confront Dewayne herself, prove she wasn't the helpless woman he believed her to be.

Perhaps her reasoning was foolish, but she needed to take control herself. Then she'd be worthy of Carson. "I can't stay with you."

"Can't, or won't?" He dropped his hand to her shoulder, and she sat up.

"Both, I guess. I can't commit, yet, and I won't put you in harm's way. Dewayne would kill you and enjoy seeing my despair."

"Do you know how emasculating that is? You, the victim, trying to protect me." He thumped his chest.

"I'm the man here. I'm supposed to be protecting you."

She chuckled. "Me Jane, you Tarzan?"

He frowned. "All right, smart ass. You know what I'm talking about."

"Yeah, I do, but in this case, facing Dewayne is something I must do. I have to stop running from him."

"Can you kill him if you have to?"

Could she? She'd fired her pistol enough to have pretty quick reflexes, but she hadn't pointed it at a human being. She snorted. Dewayne wasn't human, was he? Yeah, he was, but a poor excuse for one. He'd killed that poor woman, the mob boss's wife. He'd kill Susan too, if she let him. She didn't want to die, at least not by Dewayne's hand. If she died some other way, like in a car crash or something, she could handle it. She stifled a giggle. Like she'd know anything about it. Dead was dead. But her parents would be able to handle a car crash a lot better than death by Dewayne Holt. "Yeah, I can."

"Remember now, no time for thinking. If he confronts you, shoot first, ask questions later."

She laid her head against his chest. "I'll remember."

"By the way, who said I wanted a commitment? I just want you in my bed."

Susan jerked away from him, ready to bolt, but the goofy expression on his face stopped her. He wiggled his eyebrows.

She elbowed him in the ribs. "You masher, you."

He groaned and grabbed the offending elbow. "Now that's a word I didn't think anyone used anymore."

"Must have come from my grandmother's

vocabulary." The woman who'd instilled certain values in her, like those of home, family, and fidelity. Well, her mother had, also, but she was a bit more relaxed about today's sexual mores. "About that commitment thing, I didn't mean marriage. I meant being able to know that there would even be a relationship. I can't have sex with a man and not know if we'll be alive the next day."

His lips touched her forehead. "I know, sweetheart. I respect that about you, and commitment is important to me, too. Not to say I wouldn't jump in the sack with you at a moment's notice, but it's not a common habit for me."

She turned in his arms to face him. Her fingers brushed over the short hair at the back of his head as she pulled him closer. Their lips touched, lightly at first, easy, sampling. So sweet, yet the need for more was there waiting beneath the surface. But now was not the time. She whispered against his lips. "Soon."

Chapter Fifteen

Susan snuggled down under the covers. Sleep eluded her tonight. Thoughts of being curled against Carson's warm side invaded her thoughts. How she wanted to give in to her desire for him, let him into her bed, but desire wasn't enough. She needed to know there would be more than the moment. She'd fallen in love with him, wanted him beside her for the rest of her life, but it would kill her to endanger him even more by making him an easy target for Dewayne. Carson's offer to help her already had him in the madman's focus. If Dewayne learned of her feelings for Carson, he'd kill him just to see Susan suffer. No, she couldn't expose him further.

She sighed and stared at the ceiling. A sound from the rug by the door had her turning to see what had disturbed Hans. He stood, the ruff on his neck standing on end, as he peered at something near the fireplace. A gray mist whirled and morphed into Mr. Riley. A rumble started low in Hans's throat and blossomed into a ferocious growl. She jumped from the bed and laid a hand on the dog's back. "It's okay, boy. Meet Mr. Riley."

Hans quieted but cut a wide berth around the figure as he raised his nose to breathe in the ghost's scent. Shannon caught the light scent of tobacco. "No smoking in here, Mr. Riley."

The aroma instantly dissipated. Hans, hair still raised on his back, plunked down on his haunches between her and Mr. Riley. He no longer growled but stood guard.

"Mr. Riley, why are you visiting me? Why aren't you over there disturbing Carson's sleep?"

He chuckled. "You are more responsive to my presence." His gravelly-voiced words softly invaded the room. "You are the one who can find the Zuni treasure and return it to its rightful place."

She was more receptive? *Hmmm. Wonder why?* "So you agree it belongs with the Zuni people?"

"Yes."

"Well, where is it, then? I'm sure Carson will see it gets back to where it belongs."

"It is hidden in the mantel."

Shannon walked to the fireplace. Hans, against her legs, edged her away from Mr. Riley. She ran her hand along and underneath the heavy wood. "Where is it? I don't feel anything."

His image and voice faded. "I will come again."

"Why can't you show me now?"

"Patience, daughter." He reached toward her and a deep growl rumbled from Hans's throat. Mr. Riley chuckled. "The dog is good protection, but don't allow yourself to become complacent. It is good to see you wear White Bear. He will help you."

She clasped the fetish and, as usual, her hand warmed. Mr. Riley watched her and nodded.

"Help me what?"

"Fight the one who means you harm."

She gasped and released the bear. "How do you know about him?"

"The same way White Bear knows. We listen when the spirits talk." His voice faded into nothingness.

He was gone. Hans relaxed and padded back to his rug, where he plopped down, head on his large paws.

Susan climbed back into bed. Why did he leave without telling her where exactly in the mantel to find the treasure? Maybe his energy was restricted. Her knowledge on ghosts was limited to her childhood and what she'd seen on television. She certainly didn't believe all she saw there. Tomorrow she'd research the topic online.

The café was a hive of activity the next morning. Leona and Buck had returned from their Nashville trip. Leona rolled her eyes as Buck imitated the vocals of George Strait's "All My Exes Live in Texas." Shannon had to admit the man couldn't sing. He grabbed Leona and swung her into his version of the two-step. She pushed away and moved out of his reach. George and Carson stood behind the serving counter laughing as Buck wiggled his hips in invitation. Trying to keep a straight face, Leona swatted at him with an apron. "Get this apron on, you old fool. Let's give the kids a day off."

"Okay, my sweet dove." Leona rolled her eyes. He added, "Let's sit down and eat with the kids first, catch up on what's been happening since we've been gone." He spied Susan and made for her.

Carson reached her side first. "No, you don't, Uncle. That's my girl, and I don't share."

"Is that so?" Buck arched a shaggy brow at Shannon. "That boy telling the truth, or is he pulling this old man's leg?"

Heat rose in Susan's face. How did you answer a

question like that? Carson wrapped an arm around her shoulders. "Tell him, Shannon. There's nothing to be embarrassed about."

She leaned into Carson's side and nodded.

"Well, I'll be. How about that, Leona?"

"I could've told you that before we left." She winked at Susan. "Any fool could tell the two were sweet on each other."

"Order up," yelled George. "Shannon's breakfast is ready, Carson. Want yours now?"

Carson nudged her toward their table. "Have a seat, and I'll bring it to you." He waved at his aunt and uncle. "Y'all sit down too. We have a lot of catching up to do."

An hour later, George removed their plates while Carson refilled their coffee cups for probably the third time. Leona's forehead wrinkled in thought. She clasped Susan's hand. "What do we call you? Shannon or Susan?"

"Carson thought it'd be best to continue calling me Shannon in public, but we've decided since he knows I'm here, why continue the ruse. Call me Susan."

"I could tell you were troubled, honey, just didn't realize how bad the situation was. I told you you'd be in good hands here, didn't I?"

"Yes, you did. I'm glad I listened and came back."

"Why don't you come stay with me and Buck? Surely your ex wouldn't think to find you there."

"That's kind of you, but I'd really prefer to stay here." Susan glanced at Carson, her expression one of question. "What do you think?"

It was a possible solution, but if Dewayne wanted to get to Susan, he'd find a way, regardless of where she stayed. "No, I think she's safer here. I'm trained to protect her, and though Uncle Buck *is* pretty good with that shotgun, I don't want to see you two in danger."

Susan seemed to visibly relax in the chair beside him. He was glad she trusted him enough to prefer to stay near him.

Buck straightened in his chair. "If you need someone to stand guard, I can get some of the boys from town. We could cover the front and back of the motel day and night."

Carson stifled a shudder. The thought of some of the "boys" turned loose with rifles was worse than the thought of Dewayne and whatever weapons he might have concealed.

Buck raised a hand. "Now, I know what you're thinking, but some of the fellas served in Vietnam, and some others in Desert Storm and Iraqi Freedom. They know how to handle themselves."

Carson didn't doubt his words, but it was the few yahoos thrown into the mix he worried about. He would, however, recruit Joe. They'd served together in Afghanistan. He could trust Joe for backup in a dangerous situation. Carson didn't doubt that George, a Vietnam vet, would be good help, too. He'd talk to them both. "You're right, but I think it best we leave things as they are for right now. We don't want armed men scaring off customers, and if someone accidently got shot, we'd be in a lawsuit."

"He's right, Buck." Leona laid a hand on her husband's arm. "It's too dangerous. Carson knows what he's doing. Maybe you could bring your shotgun and leave it in the kitchen just in case of trouble."

He nodded. "I'll do it. Put it right by the back

door."

Whew! Carson was glad that was settled. "Now, we need to share something else with you." Aunt Leona sat riveted to her chair as he relayed the details about their visit to Zuni Pueblo and meeting Nona Peña.

Visibly shocked, his aunt covered her mouth with a shaking hand. Finally she spoke. "All these years we had relatives." She shook her head. "I feel we've been cheated. I'd like to meet them."

"I think that can be arranged, but first I'm going to tear this place apart until I find those ceremonial fetishes."

"We'll help you. Just tell us what to do." Leona stood. "Now, you two take the day off. Go do something fun."

"Uh, I need to tell you something first."

All eyes turned to Susan.

"I had another ghostly visit last night."

Susan's confession sent them directly to her cabin to inspect the mantel. Leona tapped gently along the entire surface. "I remember Grandpop replacing this board back in the 1950s. I was just a girl. Your mother was younger than me, Carson. She fell that day and cut her forehead on the hearth. Grandpop smoothed the edges up real nice so it wouldn't be quite as dangerous." She paused for a breath. "Of course, it'd still hurt if you fell against it, but..." She shrugged and went back to tapping on the chimneypiece. "I don't see a seam anywhere."

Buck moved her aside. "Let me have a go." His taps were hard, and Carson worried the tiles below would crack and fall.

"Not so hard. It may be that the trigger isn't even

on the mantel. It could be any one of the tiles." He turned to Shannon. "What were his exact words again?"

"He said, 'It is in the mantel.'"

In the mantel. Carson grasped the end closest to him. "Buck, you take that end. Let's see if we can lift the whole thing away from the tile. Gently. Don't yank."

It was firmly attached to either the tile or a base behind it, and no amount of jiggling and tapping would move it.

Buck strode to the door. "I'll get an axe from the utility shed."

"No!" He and Leona shouted the answer at the same time.

Lips pursed, Aunt Leona shook a finger at her husband and then pointed it at Carson, too. "I'll not allow this place to be damaged in any way. Do you understand me?"

"I agree." Carson loved the artwork his great-grandfather had created. They'd find the hidden objects somehow, but the fireplace and the ledge would be preserved.

Buck threw up his hands. "All right. You've got more patience than I do. Come on, woman, let's get back and help George."

Carson breathed a sigh of relief when they were gone. He turned to Susan. "Any ideas?"

"Nope, but he did say he'd be back, so maybe he'll tell me more then." She ran her hand lovingly over the mantel's wood. "It's so smooth. I don't see how it can open anywhere."

Frankly, Carson didn't either, but there was nothing they could do about opening it today. They'd wait to hear from Grandpop again. He restrained a guffaw and scratched his head. Here he was, considering the fact his great-grandfather had actually materialized before Susan, again. Not only appeared but talked to, again. He shrugged. His aunt and uncle didn't seem to have a problem with her story, so why should he? He gazed around the apartment. "Grandpop didn't leave another fetish, did he?"

"Nope. I looked everywhere this morning." Susan clutched the bear around her neck. "He did mention that it was good I wore White Bear, that he would help me fight Dewayne."

****

Dewayne swallowed his apprehension and parked in one of the garages, a different one this time, of the old motor court down the road from the Siesta motel. He didn't want a repeat visit from the old man. He chuckled. Almost scared the piss out of him.

He'd found a wooden crate and an old oil drum to help hoist him up to a level area on the roof of the sturdiest cottage. From there, he could watch the comings and goings of the people at the Siesta. Yeah, he'd seen his bitch of an ex-wife, along with her lover. No doubt the waitress had mentioned his visit, and they'd both be suspicious. His mug had been plastered all over the news, thanks to that waitress. Most likely his gesture to the security camera in Albuquerque didn't help, but he'd been unable to resist. No matter. He intended to wait long enough to allow Susan and Rhodes to let down their guard.

This morning some old couple showed up. They'd all gone rushing over to cabin number one—Susan's cabin. Or he should say Shannon's. Surely she didn't think changing her name would save her from his revenge. Admittedly she had eluded him for longer than he'd thought possible, but her freedom would end when she least expected it to.

The old couple came out and headed back to the restaurant. Not ten minutes later Susan, carrying a midsized purse tucked under her arm, came out with the detective, and they walked to a truck parked at the other end of the motel. They got in and drove off. Shit! By the time he got off the roof and into his little Cavalier wagon, they'd be long gone. He'd just stay up here awhile and see what went on over there. They might be back shortly. He thought about the purse. She'd never carried one of those strapless bags that you clutch in your hand or carry under the arm. She'd always favored shoulder bags, ones that held a lot of crap. Odd. Had she changed that much?

Two hours later, the truck drove back into the lot and stopped in front of Susan's cottage. Rhodes hopped out and ran around to open the door for her. Dewayne snorted. *Damn fool is besotted.* He focused the binoculars on that purse. Something about the shape had been bugging him. It was kidney shaped and zipped closed. *Well, I'll be damned.* It was a soft pistol case. His ex was packing heat. He threw back his head and laughed. His chuckle ended on an "umph" as he lost his hold on the roof and slid. He slipped down a few feet before regaining his footing, and then eased off the roof.

He rubbed his hands in glee. They'd probably been out to a shooting range somewhere. If that fool detective thought he could teach Susan enough to thwart him, he was kidding himself. She'd never get a chance to fire off a round. For that matter, neither would her lover. Dewayne was no fool, and they'd both be dead before they knew he was on them. No, that wouldn't do. He'd have to kill Rhodes. He wanted to play with Susan, make her beg before he took her life.

****

Dewayne shivered beneath the blanket he'd bought at Walmart in Gallup. He should've bought a sleeping bag, one designed for low temperatures. Trying to get comfortable, he turned onto his side. He wasn't a big man, but the fold-down back seats in his car didn't provide much room to stretch out. Plus, it was hard as hell. Even parked in the little garage, with the door down, it was too damn cold.

Revenge had its limits, even for him. Getting even could wait until it warmed up and the snow melted. She wasn't going anywhere, and with all the snow, his tire tracks and footprints were visible to anyone driving through.

Not an hour ago, he'd heard a car. Was it possible the cops were keeping an eye out for him?

Hell, the cops? How about the old man who'd visited him the other night? That was an experience he didn't want to repeat. He sat up, kicked out of the covers, and inched his way out a side door. The glow from the overhead light allowed him to find the flashlight in the front seat. With it casting a path of light across the hard-packed dirt floor, he inched his way to the old garage door. The wood creaked and the rusted metal springs popped as he pushed it up to fit against the ceiling. That it functioned after all these years remained a mystery.

A gust of wind whipped around him, and he

scurried to hop into the driver's seat. The old Cavalier engine turned over when he turned the key. Lights off, he backed out and made his way to the dilapidated two-lane road.

When he reached the access road to I-40, he flipped on the headlights and headed west. He'd make Arizona before sunrise and hole up in a motel somewhere until the weather turned warmer.

Chapter Sixteen

Susan woke warm and snug in her bed. She tried to turn over but couldn't move her feet. Hans lay curled on top of them. At her movement, he looked up and made to move. "It's okay, boy. Come on up here." Poor thing, he must have gotten cold during the night. He didn't hesitate to move up on the bed and curl up beside her. She lifted an arm from under the cover to throw over him, but yanked it back in. Dang, it was icy in here. She jumped out of bed, turned up the heat, and quickly glanced through the window. Moonlight glistened on the snow-covered ground. The neon motel sign cast a haze of green, yellow, and red across the white layer. She shook her head and grinned. The scene reminded her of striped taffy candy. She scooted under the covers and moved close to Hans's heat. The bedside clock read four a.m.—time for several more hours of sleep.

A knock on the door woke her. She rolled out of bed and peeked out the window to find Carson on the small step. Her flannel pajamas covered her from head to foot, so she opened the door. He stomped the snow from his boots and stepped inside. When his gaze raked up and down her body, the room grew considerably warmer. He leaned in and whispered against her hair, "Good morning, sleepyhead." His lips grazed her cheek and landed on her lips. "Mmm, delicious."

She covered her mouth. "Eek, my mouth feels yucky." She pulled away. "Let me run brush my teeth."

In the bathroom, she squeezed toothpaste onto her brush and started brushing, while Carson leaned against the door frame and watched. His presence didn't embarrass her or make her feel awkward, but she watched him in the mirror as he turned to the room behind him. At the sight of Hans atop her bed, his jaw dropped. He stepped toward the dog and ordered, "Down!" The dog considered him disdainfully, stretched, and rolled to his feet before hopping down. Carson turned on her, his face stern. "You can't spoil him like that. He's a guard dog, not a lap dog."

She quickly rinsed and dried her mouth and joined him. "He got cold in the middle of the night. He needs a bed of some kind, something thicker than that rug, between him and the cold floor." She wasn't about to tell him Hans had gotten on the bed without an invitation. The dog's attitude toward his master this morning was rather condescending. She didn't want to subvert any of his training and ruin Carson's hard work. Before letting him stay on the bed again, she'd think twice, but she'd make sure he had a warm place to sleep.

"Look at his thick coat, Susan. He's not going to freeze or get sick, but if it'll make you happy, I'll get him a bed."

"Good." She eyed the dog. Had he been trying to keep her feet warm last night or make himself comfortable? Oh, well, they'd never know. No doubt about it, though, the dog was smart and evidently knew how to work her. Carson was another story. And to be honest, to be dependable at his job, Hans needed a firm hand. "Yes. You're right. I shouldn't indulge him."

"I'm glad you understand." He squatted in front of the dog. "Will a nice warm bed make you happy, boy?"

Hans woofed.

"All right. Let's get outside and take care of business." The dog trotted to the door and waited while Carson turned back to her. "Can you be ready for breakfast in fifteen minutes?"

"Sure."

Business was almost non-existent at the café. Few guests visited the motel. Carson stayed open in case travelers needed a place to stay and eat, but they worked with a skeleton staff. George and Gina needed the work, so Carson took time off. He spent much of the day in her cabin studying the fireplace mantel and every piece of tile attached to the adobe structure. His strong hands smoothed, poked, and prodded each ceramic piece surrounding the hearth and every groove in the wood.

He sighed and, hands on his hips, stood back and surveyed the entire wall. "This is the damndest thing. I think it'll take a genius to figure this out." He shook his head. "I don't want to tear this wall up."

Susan didn't have a clue how to help. There had to be some simple trick, but finding it was a puzzle. They needed to know more about the man who'd designed and built it. Maybe they needed to go back to the storage shed and delve deeper into Mr. Riley's past.

"Do you still have that box of memorabilia in your cabin?"

****

An hour later the contents of several boxes from the storage building covered every available surface in

Carson's cabin. Most of it belonged to his mother and aunt—high school yearbooks, report cards, and childhood odds and ends. The only thing belonging to his great-grandfather was the deed and the sales receipts for the land he'd bought to build the motel on.

Sitting cross-legged on the floor, Susan picked through a wooden cigar box filled with old advertising giveaways—pencils, a couple of metal cigarette lighters, a fingernail file, wall thermometer, three match books, a couple of bottle openers, and numerous other items. All carried the names of businesses along Route 66. She shoved the box toward Carson. "If you have any collectors in your family, they might enjoy these."

He rifled through the contents and tossed the container onto a chair. "Uncle Buck will enjoy picking through them. He might want to put a few on display at the café."

Carson dragged another cardboard box closer and unfolded the four upper flaps. He lifted a booklet out and studied the front. "Look at this." He extended a hand from where he sat on the sofa and helped her up beside him. "I knew Sears and Wards had mail order factory homes, but this is home plans. Maybe Grandpop used these to build the first cabins."

They flipped through the book. Susan tapped a page. "Not many of these have a bathroom." She turned to the copyright page. "This was published in 1925! No bathroom. I can't believe people would build a home without one."

Carson shrugged. "Guess they were an extravagance back then."

At the very back of the book, several pieces of folded paper slid out onto his lap. He unfolded the old pages to reveal hand-drawn floor plans. In the margins, cabinets and other structures were drawn in detail. "Look, here's the tile configuration for the fireplace." He turned the page around, and on the side Mr. Riley had drawn a rough sketch of the mantel. They studied it closely.

Carson looked at Susan. "Do you see anything that hints at a secret drawer?"

"No, nothing."

****

The café bustled with activity. Susan watched as Carson, forearms crossed with elbows on the bar, chatted with a couple of regulars. The big biker, Joe, said something. Carson threw his head back and laughed. His pleasure in the exchange brought a smile to her lips. It was good to see him so happy and carefree, if only for a short while. He glanced up to see her watching and clapped the guy on the shoulder before starting toward her.

"What put that grin on your face this morning?"

"You. It's nice to see you joking around with your friends. You've been rather restrained since our visit to Zuni." Plus their search had proved fruitless.

His expression sobered as he pulled out a chair and sat. "Yeah, I'm beginning to think we'll never find the fetishes." He ran a hand through his short hair. "I hate to tear up the fireplace, but it may be the only way."

His hand, brown and strong and twice the size of hers, lay atop the table. Dark hair lightly dusted the back. She placed her pale one over his and squeezed. He clasped it, and his thumb stroked softly up and down the length of her palm. For some reason the action jolted her emotions, set butterflies loose in her stomach. She gasped.

His gaze jerked to hers. Heat and longing radiated from the dark depths of his brown eyes. He cleared his throat. "Having you here, helping, has meant a lot to me. Thank you."

"That's what friends are for, Carson. Your support these past few months has meant the world to me."

One dark brow rose. "Is that all we are to each other, Susan? Friends?" The deliberate use of her real name, though spoken softly, sent a shiver racing through her. She wanted to believe his passion, his desire for her, was something more than a passing fancy. Surely she knew his character, if not his heart, by now.

Heat rose in her face. She lowered her eyes to their joined hands. "No, we're much more than friends." She didn't intend to hedge or be coy. It wasn't in her nature. She'd not learned to play those games and didn't intend to explore the art now. She raised her head and met his gaze. "Aren't we?"

His growl rumbled softly from his chest. "Damned right."

"Hey, Carson," George called from the kitchen.

Carson frowned at the interruption, but turned. "Be right there." He stood. Her hand still in his, he pulled her to her feet. Closing the short distance between them, he cupped her cheek. "We're going to settle this tonight."

Her heart thumped rapidly in her chest. "Yes. Tonight." Fearing he'd kiss her in front of his customers, she took a step back and smiled. "Hans and I are going for a walk."

His hands dropped to cup her elbows possessively

as if willing her to stay.

"It's been a month with no sign of him."

"I don't know..."

"We'll be fine." Hans would alert her to any possible danger. "I can't stay cooped up any longer, Carson." She shrugged into her coat and patted both pockets. "I have my cell phone and my pistol."

Brows drawn together in a frown, he studied her. His attention drifted to Hans, lying on the rug beside the front door. He patted his leg. "Hans."

The dog rose and trotted over to sit in front of Carson, who voiced several commands Hans answered with a woof. Carson touched her cheek. "Be careful."

****

A knit cap pulled down to cover her ears, Susan zipped her jacket against the cold March air. Rather than put on gloves, she stuffed her hands in her pockets. She set a brisk pace and headed in a roundabout direction toward the abandoned motel. Over the past month, she and Carson had walked often, their route becoming a delineated pathway.

Susan watched Hans. Gone was the playful dog that had chased rabbits. He was all business, staying fifty yards ahead of her and occasionally stopping to lift his nose to the breeze. A true professional, the dog trotted in a zigzag pattern back and forth across the trail, stopping here and there to sniff the ground. He took his job seriously.

Though the snow had melted, small patches hid beneath shrubs, waiting for the sun to melt it away. In another month, the dry desert would awaken and signs of life would push their way through the packed earth. Plants would put on leaves and cacti would flower, adding color beneath the blue sky.

Dewayne's lack of attack was confusing. He'd never been one to let slights or wrongs go unpunished. He believed in evening the score. The longer he stayed away the more her stress increased. She was ready for the conflict to be over so she could go on with her life—if she had a life to worry about.

Tonight, Carson had said. The sensuous timbre of his voice had revealed his degree of want and determination. Yes, tonight she would tell him she loved him. No doubt they'd make love, but she wouldn't stay the night. She didn't want to be with him if Dewayne broke in. She wouldn't put him in danger. Susan couldn't bear the thought of something happening to Carson.

Susan's breath warmed the air in front of her face but not enough to warm her cheeks. The zippy weather invigorated her, and she lengthened her stride, making the muscles in her buttocks pull. She'd exercised more since coming to Siesta than she had since her teen years. Her body thrived on the activity. She slept well and had loads of energy. Her work flourished, also. Her client list had grown, and their websites kept her busy during the day. Of course, every free moment she spent with Carson. Much of that time they spent perusing his grandfather's papers. If only they could find a clue to unlock the mystery of his great-grandfather's hidden treasure...

Susan was almost to the abandoned motel, its caved-in roofs and ramshackle cottages stark against the azure backdrop of the sky. What had it been like in its heyday? Many such establishments along Route 66 had grown from mere overnight camping spots for weary travelers. Some provided no facilities, just a place to pull off the road, while a few had restrooms with showers. Regardless, they were a place to rest, build a fire and cook a meal, and visit with others on the road. She'd love to travel back in time and sit around the campfire with them, hear their stories.

Hans halted twenty yards up the trail, his snout lifted to the breeze, his attention fixed on the buildings ahead. What had caught his interest?

Light glanced off an object on the roof nearest them. Before she could react, Hans turned and moved in a blur of fur. He leapt into the air and flew, his paws catching her in the chest and knocking her to the ground just as a gunshot rang out. Her head hit a rock, and she lay there stunned, crushed under the weight of the large dog.

Chapter Seventeen

Carson chuckled at Joe's antics. The big biker, tattooed arms bare even in this cold weather, entertained Gina with his tales of exploits during his years on the road. Carson had no doubt some of the outrageous tales were true, but Joe embellished the truth. He often played the buffoon, but in truth, he was as smart as they came. His street-smart savvy served him well in a variety of situations. He was a good man to cover your back in times of trouble. They'd served in Afghanistan together back in the early 1990s, before Carson joined the force, and Joe had saved Carson's hide on more than one occasion.

Joe winked at him over Gina's head. Carson shook his own and went back to scrubbing the counter, his mind returning to Susan as it had every sixty seconds or so since she'd left. He shouldn't have let her go alone. The woman was stubborn, had a mind of her own, which he appreciated. He'd never liked clinging, needy women. Damn woman wouldn't even commit to him until this ordeal was over...if it was ever over. If they didn't catch or kill the oily bastard, he'd keep coming back like a cold sore lying dormant until you least expected it to crop up.

The echo of a rifle report startled him. Shoulders tense, he turned to Joe, hoping the sound had been his imagination. The startled expression on his friend's face erased the thought from his mind. Carson dropped the rag and rushed to the back door, Joe on his heels.

He pulled his Sig Sauer from his hidden waist holster as he ran. *Please, God, don't let me be too late.* Why had he let Susan go alone? She was an independent woman but would have listened to reason if he'd pushed the point. Would her death be another mistake to add to his conscience and haunt his dreams?

Susan liked to walk their circular route. From the amount of time she'd been gone, he calculated she'd be near the old motor court. Adrenaline rushed through his bloodstream, setting his senses on alert. The day was clear. He searched the horizon, looking for signs of Susan or Holt. A figure's head rose above the scrub brush. It was Holt, his attention trained on them. Dammit! They'd been spotted. Carson's military and police training kicked in. He signaled to Joe, and they widened the space between them and crouched low.

*****

Susan lay stunned, flat on her back, her head throbbing from where it had struck the hard ground. A heavy weight lay atop her chest. *Dang! What had happened?* She lifted her head to see Hans stretched out on top of her. She wrinkled her nose at his stinky breath and the dirty odor of his coat. *It's time for a bath, buddy.*

Reality hit. *Hans! Dewayne shot him.* She folded her arms around the animal and gasped with relief to feel his rapid pants. She stroked his side and whispered, "Lie still, boy. Play dead." Maybe he'd think he got them both.

Susan slipped the .38 revolver from her coat pocket and eased it under her right leg within easy reach. The sound of running footsteps drawing nearer alerted her to Dewayne's approach. Eyes closed, she tried to let her body go slack and pretend unconsciousness. No doubt he'd be able to see her erratic breathing under the animal. Willing it to slow, she waited.

This is it, Susan. Your chance to kill the man who beat you senseless, scarred your face, and caused all the grief you've suffered. The death of Lauren. Hate boiled inside and steadied her nerves. *Slow breath, wait…let him think you're dead or at least unconscious.*

The sounds of Dewayne's footsteps slowed, and then stopped. His harsh breathing was the only sound on the desert air. Evidently he hadn't kept in shape and his run had winded him. Slight noises rustled from another direction. His position had shifted. Damn, he was suspicious and approaching cautiously. She forced herself to keep her eyes closed and still.

Cold steel touched her forehead. She popped her eyes open and allowed her gaze to travel up the length of the rifle barrel. She stared at the grinning face of her archenemy, only he was no longer the handsome man she'd known. His face wasn't badly scarred, but the lack of eyebrows and lashes made his cold eyes radiate even more malice. The dark-rimmed glasses with their thick lenses tripled the size of the blue orbs.

"Can't fool me, bitch! You were always good at playing possum." He nudged Hans with his boot.

The dog whined but didn't attempt to move.

Susan feared he was severely wounded, else he'd already have attacked Dewayne. From the amount of warm wetness seeping into her clothes, he was bleeding badly and the wound needed immediate attention for him to survive.

"Get up," Dewayne ordered.

Play for time, Susan. Carson has to have heard the gunshot and will be on his way. She pretended to try to ease Hans off her. "I can't. He's too heavy."

The sound of a hammer being pulled back drew her eyes to Dewayne's left hand and a .45 revolver. He aimed for Hans's head. "Either move the damn dog or I'll make sure he's dead."

"No! I'll try harder." If only she could ease her hand back under her for the gun before Dewayne could follow through on his threat. Her fingers inched toward her leg.

"I mean it, Susan. He's just a mangy animal."

Shouts rang out across the desert from the direction of the Siesta Motel. *Carson. And thank God he wasn't alone.*

With a booted foot, Dewayne rolled Hans off her. He pocketed the revolver and with his left hand grabbed the front of her jacket and yanked her up. Her hand fumbled for her .38 but she stumbled and dropped it. She cried out in frustration.

A bullet whizzed past Dewayne's head. He cursed and dragged her along toward the abandoned buildings.

"Susan! Down!" Carson's voice carried across the distance. Remembering her training, she dropped to the dirt, breaking Dewayne's grasp on her. The loose rocks scraped her hands and knees.

Dewayne stopped and bent to grab her. His head jerked up at the sound of gunfire. Bullets flew past his head. He ducked and hunched his shoulders. "I'll get you, Susan," he shrieked as he turned and ran.

Susan scrambled back for her revolver. She rose to her knees, took aim and fired. "Take that, you sorry son-of-a-bitch." She aimed for his back. "Run, you coward!"

He stumbled. Had she hit him? He glanced over his shoulder to see her taking aim again, ducked his head, and broke into a shuffling run.

She shot the remaining four rounds in her Smith and Wesson but missed him.

More voices joined Carson's. "She got him," hollered one of the men.

Carson dropped to the dirt beside her, hands gripping her shoulders. "Oh, God. You're covered in blood?" His hands skimmed her body, checking for wounds, while George and Joe continued to chase after Dewayne.

"No, no. This is Hans's blood." She gingerly touched the back of her head. It was sore, but no skin was broken.

"Thank God." He held her close, his breath warm against her hair.

"But..." Her voice broke. "Hans is hurt pretty bad."

Jaw rigid, he rose and pulled her to her feet. They hurried to Hans and dropped beside him. Carson's hands roamed lovingly over the animal and carefully turned him to expose a bleeding hole in his abdomen. Voice thick with held-in emotion, Carson crooned, "It's going to be okay, boy. We'll get you to the doc." He rubbed Hans's head. "You did a fine job, boy. You protected Susan."

Hans, his breathing rapid, whined and licked Carson's hand. His eyes rolled back in his head, and he quieted. Carson felt for a pulse and breathed, "He's still alive."

George and Joe returned. "Sorry, Carson, he got in

that little car and hightailed it out of here. Cut across the field to the interstate. Didn't even take the main road." Joe guffawed. "Bet his tires will be a mess and he won't get far."

George dropped beside them and touched Hans. "Ah, man. He's not dead, is he?"

Carson shrugged out of his jacket. "No, but he could die at any minute. I need to get him to the vet. Help me slide him onto my jacket."

When Hans was wrapped up, Carson lifted the bundle and carried him back to the café. Susan held the truck door while he slid in with Hans cradled against his chest. She climbed behind the wheel and, throwing gravel, sped off toward Siesta and the veterinary clinic. George had called ahead, and Dr. Juarez had the surgery ready.

Joe had contacted the police, and a manhunt was underway. Undoubtedly Dewayne would need medical care; their bullets had hit him at least once. If he turned up at an area hospital, he'd be arrested. While she waited for Carson to return to the waiting room, a local police officer arrived to take her statement. She couldn't tell him much. Hopefully Joe or George would be able to identify the type of car Dewayne had been driving.

Two hours later, Carson came into the lobby. His face haggard, he smiled and pulled her into his arms. "He's going to make it, but he'll need to stay here overnight."

She sagged with relief. "I'm so glad."

His hand cupped her cheek as he peered down at her. "I'm going to stay with him for awhile, but I'll be at your place later tonight. I'll have Joe and George keep an eye on you until I can get there."

"There is no need. I'll be fine. You stay with Hans." After all, she'd winged Dewayne. "I doubt Dewayne will be up to coming after me tonight."

"I don't know. The man's not done anything like we thought he would." His brow furrowed. "Maybe you should go stay with Aunt Leona and Uncle Buck until I can pick you up."

She didn't want to go somewhere else. The little cottage had become home, and that's where she wanted to be. "I'll be fine, Carson." She smiled up at him, hoping to ease his worry. "You concentrate on Hans. Do you need anything from home, like a shave kit or clean underwear?"

He grinned and tweaked her nose. "Haha, very funny. I don't think they have human showers here, and I don't intend to get in the dog bath."

"How will you get home?"

"I'll have someone bring my pickup back and leave it out front."

Carson walked her to the truck. She slid behind the wheel, and to her surprise he opened the passenger door and got in beside her. Arm around her shoulders, he tugged. "Come here, woman."

She moved to snuggle against him. He tilted her face to his and traced her lips with a finger. "You scared the devil out of me earlier. I don't know what I'd have done if Dewayne had killed you. I think I aged ten years."

"Well, I was rather terrified myself."

"You did really well, sweetheart. I'm proud of how you handled yourself." He chuckled. "Guess we know you can shoot someone if you have to."

"Surprised you, huh? Surprised myself, too." But she'd not thought twice about firing at Dewayne. She guessed her self-preservation instinct took over.

"I had hoped tonight we'd be together in my bed, skin to skin." He yanked on her coat. "Not with all these layers between us."

His words sent fire to her belly. She longed for the same thing, being with this man, fully. "Uh, well, sorry about that." Her heart thumped rapidly in her chest. She tugged his mouth down to hers and whispered against it. "I'd rather hoped for the same thing."

A groan rumbled from his chest. "I love you, Susan. I want you to marry me and us to build a life together." He wiggled his eyebrows. "And I want to have sex with you every morning and night."

She wanted that too, but feared he would be disappointed after they made love. Dewayne had been. Said she was a cold bitch. Well, after his foray into drugs, that is. "I don't want to disappoint you, Carson."

"You cannot disappoint me, Susan. Your body responds to mine, as mine does to yours. Together we'll set the sheets on fire...or the kitchen table...or—"

"Yikes! Enough." Her face burned, and no doubt he could see her embarrassment.

He nuzzled the sensitive spot below her ear. "Don't be embarrassed, sweetheart." He kissed his way to her lips. "Kiss me now before I go back inside."

When he released her, they both gasped for air. "Still have doubts?"

She grinned. "No."

He slid across the seat and out of the cab. "Be careful. See you in the morning."

"I will." She started the truck. "And Carson, I love

you too."

Chapter Eighteen

Though Hans never made much noise, the lack of the dog's company caused Susan some disquiet. From her spot in the middle of the bed, she glanced toward the huge pillow Carson had purchased as a bed for Hans. The plaid flannel cushion took up an immense amount of space beside her bed. Every time she got up, she had to watch her step to keep from tripping over it. Hans had immediately known the pad was for him. He'd stepped into the middle, turned around several times, and plunked down. Susan grinned at the memory.

Carson had asked, "Does it meet with your approval, boy?"

A woof had been his answer.

Susan glanced around the room. She wasn't afraid, more like lonely, missed the click of Hans's nails, his scratching, his snuffling snore at night. Anyway, Dewayne was probably holed up somewhere nursing his wounds. Had he found medical care, or would he have patched himself up in fear of being arrested if he visited a hospital? No telling. With his connections, he might be in a facility being pampered this very minute. Regardless, he wouldn't be on her doorstep.

She closed her laptop and reached to set it on the bedside table. Her revolver lay within easy reach, as did her cell phone. She turned out the reading light and snuggled down under the covers. Her eyes adjusted to the darkness. She watched little flickers of light from the headlights on the interstate dance by on the shiny tiles of the fireplace. Why hadn't Mr. Riley been back to give them further clues to the treasure? Carson had been thrilled to find the house plans, especially those with notes all over them. They'd even come across a sketch for the tile arrangement and the mantel, but it offered no hints on a secret compartment.

"Where are you, Mr. Riley?" The quiet continued. "Your great-grandson needs your help, you know. By the way, he met your wife's sister, Nona. What a shame Lily and Nona never saw each other again. Of course, Nona was very small at the time, but even though your wife's name was never spoken again, Nona remembered her big sister."

Susan yawned, ending in an "ohhh" as she fell asleep.

****

A sound woke her. Cold air brushed against her cheek. She lay still, thinking. Seemed Mr. Riley must have heard her earlier and decided to show himself. Why couldn't he have come while she was awake? She sniffed the air, seeking the faint scent of tobacco, but instead of its sweet fragrance she caught a whiff of something rancid, dirty. She stiffened and reached for her revolver.

"Don't move." She heard a menacingly familiar cackle and the slap of a hand against cloth. "I've got your little gun in my pocket here."

She froze and rolled to her back to face her intruder. Praying it wasn't Dewayne would be useless, but a plea for help might work. *Lord, please help me live*. Her heart thudded against her chest, making breathing difficult. Her hands shook as she pressed them against the mattress and scooted up in the bed to lean against the headboard. *Calm down, Susan. Don't let him see your fear.*

"What? No shrieks of fear, pleas for your life?" He glanced around the dark room, dimly lit by moonlight and the neon signs outside. "Where's your lover?"

He stood two feet from the bed, a gun aimed in her direction. Why wasn't he licking his wounds somewhere?

Anger rose inside her over what he'd done to Hans, what he'd tried to do to her. "He's at the animal hospital with Hans. The dog is going to recover."

"Ah, how sweet." He shrugged. "I wasn't aiming for him, but the mutt got in the way."

"You better pray he never sees you again, because he'll tear you into little pieces—so fast you'll never see him coming."

"Shut up. I don't like your lippy attitude. Liked you better when you were a scaredy-cat."

"Guess you beat it all out of me, Dewayne."

"Well, after tonight I won't have to worry about it any longer." He walked to the end of the bed, his limp making his progress slow. How had she missed his shuffling gait, not heard him, when he came in? It must be the pain medication she'd taken.

"I hope your leg develops gangrene, rots off, and you die writhing in pain. I'll be in heaven watching and laughing the entire time."

"You bitch!" He limped back to the side of the bed and hit her on the side of the face with his pistol. Pain sliced through her as bone cracked, and she feared he'd broken her cheekbone again. She stifled a scream. "I'm going to mess you up before I shoot you. Give that boyfriend something to remember me by."

She gasped around her agony and panted out, "You always were a sissy, Dewayne, getting your jollies beating up defenseless people, like women. Now that you've lost your good looks, have you started abusing children yet?"

****

The bitch had grown a mouth. Dewayne had liked her better when she was meek and scared. He wanted his hands around her throat. Then she'd lose some of that mouthy attitude. He yelled and lunged for her, but hit a solid wall. Something—something invisible—kept him from moving.

"What the hell?" He tried again. Whatever it was pushed him backward. He stumbled and ended up lying across the bed. Susan snatched at the gun, trying to wrestle it away from him. They grappled for the revolver, and he snatched it from her grasp and swung, barely missing her. "You bitch."

He bounded upright and turned on Susan. Pain shot up his leg to his hip. Gasping, he gritted his teeth to keep from screaming.

Susan leapt to her feet and ran across the mattress and onto the floor toward the bathroom. He stumbled after her, desperate to catch her. Again he hit a solid wall. Swinging his arms, he fought to gain purchase with the unseen force but kept stumbling back toward the fireplace. What the hell was going on here? Was this some kind of new secret weapon?

Suddenly the pressure eased, and he limped forward, pistol aimed at her back. She was scrambling to get something from the medicine cabinet. He chuckled. Did she plan to blind him with hairspray? His life was over. He'd killed a woman, and the cops would find him eventually. If she thought a little aerosol spray could save her, she'd better rethink her plan.

At last, bitch. Turn around. I want to see the fear in your eyes when I kill you. Susan turned, a small handgun in her hand pointed at his heart. He roared with laughter. Yeah, she'd shot him while he'd been running, but to his face? He choked on his guffaw as a figure—a man—took shape beside her. *What the hell...?* It was the Indian man, the one who'd visited him at the abandoned motel, dressed in full warrior regalia, his tomahawk raised with savage intent. *No, no way... Ghosts don't exist... I'm hallucinating from the pain.* He shook his head to clear his vision and pointed his gun at Susan. His hand shook so hard his teeth clacked against each other.

The ghost spoke, and his guttural voice froze Dewayne in place.

****

"Be strong, woman. Remember you wear White Bear. He will give you courage." Mr. Riley had spoken out loud, and from the expression on Dewayne's face, her ex not only saw him but heard him, as well. Dewayne, eyes round with shock, started backing up.

"Mr. Riley?" She clasped the fetish that dangled from rawhide around her neck. The bear warmed in her hand, reminding her to be strong.

"You must do it, Daughter."

Susan didn't have to ask what Mr. Riley meant. She pointed the Ruger and fired all seven rounds into Dewayne. Each one sent him closer to the fireplace, until he crashed into it and slid to the ground in a heap. Smears of blood distorted the beautiful tiles.

Pounding on the door and someone yelling, "Susan, Susan!" drew her eyes from the grisly scene. A loud crash followed as the door burst in. It was Joe and George. One of them flipped the light switch. She squinted against the glare and looked to see if Mr. Riley still stood beside her. He was gone.

Joe carefully approached and took the Ruger from her trembling hand. "Damn, your face is bleeding. Are you hurt anywhere else?"

She shook her head. Her face throbbed. She reached a trembling hand up to touch her cheek and winced.

George put his arms around her and hugged. "You did good, girl. Real good. The medics will be here in a minute to patch you up." He patted her back. "Cry now if you want. It's okay. Carson is on his way."

She trembled in George's arms but no tears came. Within minutes Carson burst through the door. She fell against his chest, and then sobs erupted, tears of cleansing release. Her outburst didn't last long, but the shakes continued. She didn't regret killing Dewayne but resented the circumstances making it necessary. He'd never have left her in peace; even behind prison walls, he'd have found a way to torment her.

Carson held her, nestled her head against his neck, and murmured words of comfort. Finally, she asked, "How'd you get here so fast?"

He grinned and glanced over his shoulder. "Joe called. Then I heard the police sirens. I was in the truck on my way home when they rushed by."

Susan looked around him at the men filing into the

room. A couple of them stepped around the body, taking notes, while one stood at the door to keep curiosity seekers away. Dewayne remained upright, sitting slumped on the hearth, seeming to be in the process of sliding off yet staying as he'd landed. In death, his eyes fixed on some distant spot, he appeared harmless, but she shivered and turned away. Carson grabbed a blanket from the closet shelf and wrapped it around her shoulders.

He led her to the bed. "Crawl in and get under the covers." He propped two pillows behind her head and pulled the blanket up under her arms. "The detectives will want to take your statement here in a minute." He sat on the side of the bed facing her, one hand propped beside her hip. With the other he examined the wound on her face. She jerked back when he touched it. "I'm sorry."

"It's sore."

"The medics will be here in a minute to take care of it." He tucked her loose hair behind her ear. "How do you feel?"

She didn't think he was referring to her head. "Fine, I think, but it does hurt."

"Can I get you anything?"

"Maybe a couple of aspirin." Her cheek throbbed. She reached up to touch the spot, but Carson caught her hand.

"Let's wait on the paramedics. They'll want to see you first, and then they'll give you something." He smiled, but the expression didn't reach his eyes. "And you're not fine, sweetheart. You're probably in shock, and reality will set in later. Seasoned police officers experience trauma after killing someone, even when it's self-defense." His lips brushed hers. "I won't leave you."

She sniffed and brushed back a tear. "Okay." He moved closer to her and wrapped her in his arms. The steady thump of his heart and his strength reassured her. She gripped the fabric of his jacket to keep him close.

He cupped the back of her head and turned his face into her hair. "Oh, Lord, when I got the call that shots had been fired, I about died of a heart attack on the spot. I should have been here with you."

"We had no way of knowing Dewayne would come tonight. He was shot, for gosh sake. Hans needed you. Plus you needed to be with him, to oversee his recovery." She placed her lips against his ear. "Anyway, I had backup."

He tilted his head back, his gaze questioning. "You mean Joe and George?"

"No. Mr. Riley."

He released her. His eyes widened. "No!"

"Yes! He reminded me I had a backup plan, or I wouldn't have remembered the gun in my medicine cabinet. And Carson, Dewayne saw the ghost... He heard him. Mr. Riley scared the bejeebers out of Dewayne."

George tapped Carson on the shoulder and nodded toward the fireplace. "Take a look. I think Dewayne found your Grandpop's treasure."

Sure enough, a small drawer had popped out of the tiles just below the mantel.

****

Detectives Haney and Williams arrived along with a coroner's van from Albuquerque. Haney shook Carson's hand and nodded to Susan before turning to chat with the local police officers. Williams took note of the scene and then watched as the medical examiner checked Dewayne's body. He and one of the local detectives, Steve Greyhawk, strode over. The older man grasped Carson's hand. "Howdy, Carson."

"Greyhawk."

He squatted before Susan. "Detective Greyhawk, ma'am." He glanced at her bandaged cheek and then at her trembling shoulders. "You feel up to answering a few questions?"

"Yes. I'd like to get this over with." She glanced at Dewayne's body and shuddered.

"That'd be very helpful, ma'am." He turned to Carson. "Can we go somewhere else to talk? It's too crowded in here."

Carson couldn't agree more. Susan needed to get away from the gruesome scene. "Good idea." He helped her up. "Why don't you grab some clothes and your computer? This room may be off limits for several days."

Within minutes, Susan sat on his couch, her feet drawn up beneath her, her hands wrapped around a mug of hot tea. Carson settled beside her. Williams sat in a chair across from them, Greyhawk next to him in a kitchen chair. "As a courtesy to the Chicago PD, we're allowing them to observe this investigation. Any objections?"

Susan shook her head and looked at Carson for confirmation.

"None. How'd you get here so fast, Williams?" Carson asked.

"Captain Farley notified us that Holt had been spotted." He nodded to Susan. "And that you'd winged him. When we heard, we boarded a plane for Albuquerque. Received a call at the airport about the break-in and shooting tonight. Hopped an Albuquerque police helicopter and flew straight here."

Greyhawk added, "We've been in close contact with Albuquerque PD since Holt's first appearance here at the café. Thought he might hide out at the old motel down the road, so we've been making surveillance drives through the area. But we don't have a large staff. If we had, perhaps we could have prevented today's earlier occurrence." He flipped open a note pad. "Now, Miss Lawton, let's start from the beginning."

****

The sound of Susan's soft snuffle in her sleep comforted Carson. If he had anything to do with it, she'd be in his bed from now on. He loved her, wanted her to marry him. Would she be able to commit now that Dewayne was dead?

She lay curled on her side, one hand under her cheek, the one not patched up with gauze. Thank goodness the bone wasn't broken. She'd be mighty sore for several days, and bruised, but those wounds would heal without permanent results. Killing someone was a different story. Some people never got over it. She'd seemed fine before falling asleep. It's possible her survival instinct would prevent her from beating herself up over DeWayne's death. Yes, she could have just wounded him, but the man held a gun. He could have still shot her. She had no choice but to empty her gun into him.

Barefoot, Carson padded softly to the closet to hang up his coat. In the soft glow from the kitchenette, his gaze fell on the old coat hanging to the side. He'd noticed it before, an old bomber jacket, and had explored all the pockets over a month ago. But someone, maybe Susan, had moved it to a more prominent position. A chill permeated the closet, and he shivered. He glanced at Susan to see if she was well covered. Drawn by an invisible force, he reached toward the cracked leather and fished through the left and then the right pocket. His hand closed on a small cloth bag. He emptied the contents into his hand. The stone pieces rattled against each other as they hit his palm. An eerie sound reverberated through the closet at his discovery. It resembled a grateful sigh, one echoing from deep within someone's chest—Grandpop's chest.

****

Mr. Peña and the tribal elders waited for them at the meeting lodge in Zuni. Mr. Zeekya greeted them at the door. "I'm sorry to hear of your tragedy, Miss Lawton, but I'm glad the evil man will bother you no more."

"Thank you. I'm glad it's all over and I can now move on with my life."

"Come, Nephew," called Aunt Nona from across the room. "Show us what you found."

Carson placed a basket on the table. His audience leaned forward as he unwrapped its contents to reveal the prayer fetishes. He lifted a yellow mountain lion, representing north, and placed it on the table. "Ahs" accompanied each fetish—the blue-black bear—west, the red badger—south, the white wolf—east, the multicolored eagle—the sky, and the mole—the underground.

Carson observed the group as they gazed on the fetishes, reverence evident in their expressions. This collection was not like the tiny objects left for him and Susan. He'd found the rest of that small collection in the pockets of the old jacket belonging to his Grandpop. Though old, they couldn't compare to this antique set. These were larger and cruder carvings.

Mr. Peña nodded to Carson and cleared his throat. His deep voice thick with emotion, he said, "Carson Rhodes, we are grateful to you for returning these valued relics to our safe keeping. The Zuni people thank you."

Heart in his throat, Carson gathered his emotions before speaking. "I'm sorry it took so long to return them. I do believe Grandpop regretted keeping them. On his deathbed, he tried to tell Granddad about them, but his delirious raving didn't make sense at the time." It must have struck a chord though, for his grandfather did begin a search.

Nona lifted one of the crudely shaped carvings. Though primitive compared to the modern art pieces, there was no denying which animal each symbolized. Tears glistened in her eyes. "I thought never to see these again."

Mr. Peña patted her hand. "They are home now, Mother. We will guard them well." Carson had suspected at their first meeting that the man might be an uncle, but having it confirmed was a shock.

Mr. Peña must have noticed the stunned expression on Carson's face. He smiled. "Yes, Carson, I am your uncle."

"Do I have other relatives here at Zuni?"

The older man laughed, his dark eyes lit with humor, deepening the already-deep wrinkles of his brown skin, a stark contrast to his white hair. "At least fifty, Nephew. We will introduce you one day soon. Perhaps you and Miss Lawton will return in December for the winter solstice celebration ceremonies."

Carson clasped Susan's shoulder. "How about it?"

"I'd love to." She turned to Mr. Peña. "Is this when the fetishes will be blessed?"

"Yes. We don't usually allow outsiders to attend, but I think we can make an exception for you." He waved at the two vacant chairs. "Sit. We are anxious to hear of your latest adventure with Mr. Riley's ghost."

Chapter Nineteen

It was after dark when they arrived at the Inn at Halona, a bed and breakfast one block from Zuni Pueblo, the only lodgings at Zuni. They'd settled into their room earlier. Susan loved the roughhewn furniture and woven Aztec rugs. She glanced at the queen-sized bed. Though she'd shared Carson's bed the past two nights, he'd done nothing more than hold her to ease her shakes. Her gut told her tonight would be different. It was time. Carson had been more than patient with her, accepting her reasons for waiting. Few men would have, another indication of his strong character.

Carson placed two grocery sacks on the small table. From one he lifted two bowls and a sack of dog food. With a glance at Hans lying on his bed at the foot of theirs, he asked, "You ready to eat, boy?" The dog pushed to his feet and walked to his bowl. Carson spooned out some wet canned food and mixed it with the dry food. "Now, don't get used to this nasty canned stuff, boy. This is only until you get well." Hans snuffled and munched away.

Susan emptied the other bag, laying out a cheese/meat/fruit tray and opening a box of crackers. They'd purchased the items in the store next door to the inn. The beer and wine they'd brought from home. "I thought there would be glasses in the room, but I can't find any."

"I'll run over to the main building and see if they have a couple."

He returned with two wine goblets. "You want wine or beer?"

"Wine."

He poured two glasses of the red and handed her one. She took a sip. It eased smoothly down her throat, leaving a trail of warmth in its wake. "Mmm, nice."

"Very! I'll have to remember this brand."

****

Susan sat in bed reading a brochure on the Zuni area when Carson emerged from the bathroom. Previously he'd worn a T-shirt with his pajama bottoms, but tonight he was shirtless and the pants rode low on his hips. Her breath hitched in her chest. *Oh, my, he's a beautiful man.* His muscled chest, arms, and abdomen rippled as he padded barefoot across the room. She dared not look lower to see the state of anything else. Her mouth watered in anticipation of touching his bronzed skin, feeling its texture under her hands. She'd touched it before, but tonight was different.

"What're you reading?" He turned out the overhead light and crawled into bed beside her. Propped on one elbow, he faced her.

"A pamphlet about the area. There's a lot to see."

He took the paper and gave it a cursory glance. "One day we'll come back and take in the sights." He reached across her and shut off the lamp. His breath whispered across her cheek and he pulled her closer. "Right now, I want to love you."

"I want that too." She tilted her face to his. Their lips met. His tasted and teased. Heat bloomed in her belly, and her heart swelled with love for this man. She shivered and melted against his hard length, aching to get closer. As his hands stroked her body, she learned the texture and strength of his. Their breaths and sighs mingled in the dark. When he entered her, she reveled in the fulfillment, her joy burst around her, and she wept against Carson's neck.

****

Carson cradled Susan close. Her breath whispered across his cheek. They lay facing, legs twined, bodies sated from their lovemaking. Contrary to Susan's fear, he wasn't disappointed in her response. She'd blushed afterward and said, "I don't know what came over me."

He was unable to resist laughing outrageously. She swatted him on the belly, but he captured her hand and pulled her close again. "Maybe it's because I know how to love you."

She'd smiled. "Maybe."

He sighed, content to have this woman beside him. Hans yawned on his bed on the floor and uttered a snort. "I know, fella, I'm one happy, boring man."

****

Susan had met and conquered her demons. Now she insisted he do the same.

Inside New Mexico Women's Correctional Facility in Grants, Carson was searched before being admitted to the visitation room. His stomach knotted with tension. It had been two years since he'd last seen Trina Washington. That day in court she'd been distraught, her health fragile from years of drug use. Her hate-filled eyes had speared him as the officers pulled her from the room. She'd screamed, "Murderer! You killed my baby...my baby...Oh, God..." Would her screams haunt him forever?

He shivered and sat down. Trina blamed him, and it was time to meet her face-to-face and ask her forgiveness. The sound of large keys in a heavy metal door and the buzz of its alarm interrupted his thoughts. He glanced up to see a guard escort an attractive dark-skinned woman through the door. Clean and neat, her orange jumpsuit enhanced her coffee-colored skin. She smiled at Carson and started his way.

"Trina?"

"I know. You didn't recognize me, did you?"

"To be honest, no." This woman's skin was clear, her hair shiny, her teeth fixed. No doubt the citizens of New Mexico had paid for that, but if this woman left prison with a new attitude and purpose in life, it was worth it, in his opinion.

She settled in a chair. "I barely recognize myself sometimes."

He sat across from her and folded his hands on the table, struggling for the right words. She reached for his hand and gripped it tightly.

"You don't have to say it, Detective."

Voice choked, he said, "Yes, I do...to eradicate the ghosts and clear my conscience. Not that mere words will be enough, but I truly am sorry I fired the shot that killed your daughter." He coughed to clear his throat. "She was a precious child, and her death will haunt me for the rest of my life."

Tears flowed down Trina's cheeks, and she wiped at them with her free hand. "Yes, she was." Her chin wobbled, and she bit her bottom lip to steady the trembling. "Her death is my fault, not yours. If I hadn't been involved with drugs, you wouldn't have had to bust into my home." Her eyes, dark with sorrow, pleaded with him to understand. "I killed my child, not you. I deal with it every day, and hopefully one day I'll be able to forgive myself."

As Carson walked back to the van, his heart lightened, but he grieved for Trina Washington. He couldn't imagine what she suffered. She'd offered him forgiveness and solace. He wished he could do the same for her. Hopefully in time she'd accept society's forgiveness, and God's, and be able to forgive herself. Then she might be able to start anew.

Hans thumped his tail in greeting when he entered the camper van. Susan lay curled up on the bed. He kicked off his shoes and slipped in beside her.

She turned and snuggled against him. "How did it go?"

"Good. Really well." He breathed in her subtle perfume.

Her arms tightened, drawing him closer. She stroked his back. "I'm so glad." Her touch soothed him further. He longed to close his eyes and drift to sleep. Better yet, strip her and make love to her.

"She blames herself for her daughter's death, not me." He hurt for the woman.

"Poor thing. Drugs destroyed her life, just as they put Dewayne on the road to destruction."

He tucked a tendril of hair behind her ear. "Let's not dwell on the past. We have an entire future to think about."

She yawned and stretched, then cast him a sexy smile.

He sat up and bent to pick up a shoe. "Hey, woman, don't look at me like that. We need to travel at least a hundred miles, two if possible, before stopping for the night. Your folks will be disappointed if we're late arriving in Chicago."

"Yeah, I know." She rolled to her knees and laid her head against his back. "I can't wait to see them." Arms around his chest, she squeezed. "And on the way back, driving Route 66 will be so much fun."

"Don't forget, we need at least a week to settle into our house in Albuquerque before I go back to work."

He turned and lifted her onto his lap. "Are you sure you don't mind me going back to detective work?"

"You've told me every horror story you could think of, Carson, but it's your life, and I won't keep you from doing what makes you happy." She stroked his cheek. "We'll be fine."

God, he hoped so. Dewayne was dead. Hopefully Carson had buried his demons. He'd know soon enough.

"All right, wife. Let's hit the road."

She giggled. "Yes, dear."

References

Books

Cushing, Frank Hamilton. *Zuni Fetishes.* Las Vegas, Nevada: KC Publications, 1994.

Kelly, Susan Croce. *Route 66, The Highway and Its People.* Norman and London, Oklahoma: University of Oklahoma Press, 1991.

McManis, Kent. *Zuni Fetishes & Carvings One Volume, Expanded Edition.* Tucson, Arizona: Rio Nuevo Publishers, 2004.

Snyder, Tom. *Route 66 Travelers Guide and Roadside Companion Collector's Edition.* New York: St. Martin's Griffin, 2000.

Websites

"About Fetishes—Zuni Fetish Meanings." Zuni Fetishes Direct, Gallup, New Mexico.
http://www.zunifetishesdirect.com/about.htm

"Zuni Fetishes and Carvings Old and New." Horsekeeping LLC, USA.
http://www.horsekeeping.com/jewelry/Fetish-about-page1.htm

"Zuni Fetishes. A little history about Zuni Fetishes you may find interesting." Indian Summer Native American Art, Salt Lake City, Utah.
http://www.indiansummer.com/fetishes.htm.

"Information On The Zuni Indian Tribe." Essortment, Your Source for Knowledge.
http://www.essortment.com/information-zuni-indian-tribe-63766.html

"Zuni Fetishes." Wikipedia.
http://en.wikipedia.org/wiki/Zuni_fetishes

A word about the author...

Linda LaRoque is a Texas girl, but the first time she got on a horse, it tossed her in the road, dislocating her right shoulder. Forty years passed before she got on another, but it was older, slower, and she was wiser. Plus, her students looked on, and it was important to save face.

A retired teacher who loves West Texas, its flora and fauna, and its people, Linda's stories paint pictures of life, love, and learning set against the raw landscape of ranches and rural communities in Texas and the Midwest. She is a member of RWA, her local chapter of HOTRWA, NTRWA, and Texas Mountain Trail Writers.

Susan lay stunned, flat on her back, her head throbbing from where it had struck the hard ground. A heavy weight lay atop her chest. *Dang! What had happened?* She lifted her head to see Hans stretched out on top of her. She wrinkled her nose at his stinky breath and the dirty odor of his coat. *It's time for a bath, buddy.*

Reality hit. *Hans! Dewayne shot him.* She folded her arms around the animal and gasped with relief to feel his rapid pants. She stroked his side and whispered, "Lie still, boy. Play dead." Maybe he'd think he got them both.

Susan slipped the .38 revolver from her coat pocket and eased it under her right leg within easy reach. The sound of running footsteps drawing nearer alerted her to Dewayne's approach. Eyes closed, she tried to let her body go slack and pretend unconsciousness. No doubt he'd be able to see her erratic breathing under the animal. Willing it to slow, she waited.

This is it, Susan. Your chance to kill the man who beat you senseless, scarred your face, and caused all the grief you've suffered. The death of Lauren. Hate boiled inside and steadied her nerves. *Slow breath, wait...let him think you're dead or at least unconscious.*

The sounds of Dewayne's footsteps slowed, and then stopped. His harsh breathing was the only sound on the desert air. Evidently he hadn't kept in shape and his run had winded him. Slight noises rustled from another direction. His position had shifted. Damn, he was suspicious and approaching cautiously. She forced herself to keep her eyes closed and still.

Cold steel touched her forehead.

Praise for *A STOLEN CHANCE*

"From the first page, *A STOLEN CHANCE* drew me in with its suspense. Linda LaRoque painted a fatally flawed ex-husband who'd strike fear in any woman's heart, so I cheered the heroine's bravery and ingenuity in staking her claim to independence and freedom. Like Susan, I fell in love with Carson, the hero, and it was so satisfying when the warmth between them grew into a steady flame.

"The light mix of Zuni history, magic, ghosts, and legends lent mystique to the story. I loved that every character found the healing, or punishment, each needed. Even Carson's dog Hans is an unforgettable character.

"After devouring *A STOLEN CHANCE* in one sitting, I highly recommend it. This is one trip down Route 66 you won't soon forget!"

~Multi-published, award-winning author Cate Masters

~*~

"Miss LaRoque's blending of modern day suspense with the historical aspects of Native American cultures makes for an interesting read."

~P. L. Parker, Romantic Adventure at its Best